GORGRON
THE DARK MAGE

KHRIS SMITH

INDEPENDENTLY PUBLISHED

Contents

Prologue	1
1. Chapter One	5
2. Chapter Two	31
3. Chapter Three	43
4. Chapter Four	61
5. Chapter Five	83
6. Chapter Six	91
7. Chapter Seven	113
Epilogue	131
About the Author	139
Acknowledgments	140

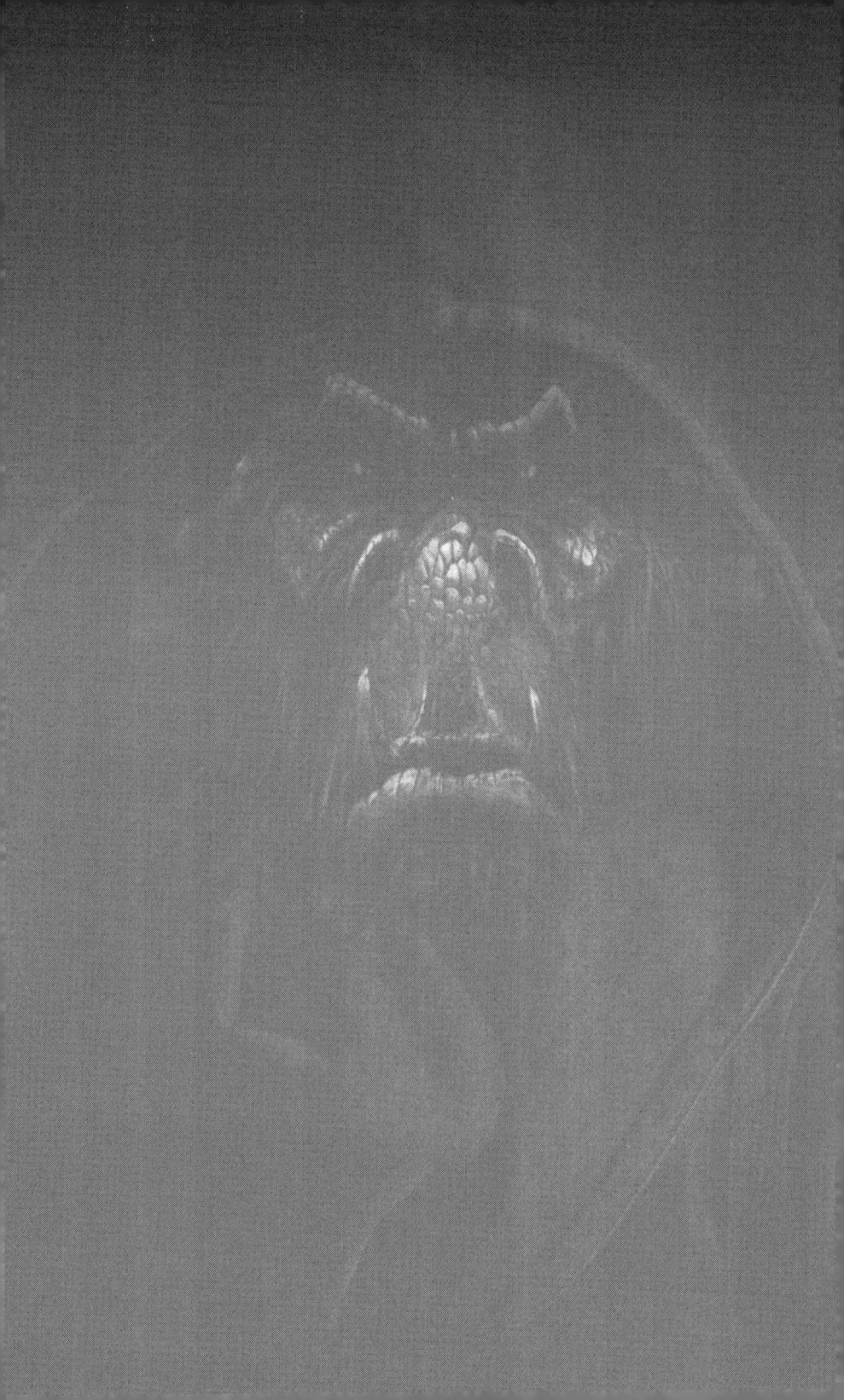

PROLOGUE

It was around two months ago that he wandered into town. The shadows of his brown cloak obscured his face from most of the townsfolk's view. It was rare that any of them got to see an orc. The sight of his broad shoulders, gray skin, and thick tusks that jutted out from the corners of his lower lip was enough to put most of the townspeople on guard. The majority of their dealings with orcs had been temporary and were few and far between. Usually, they were just travelers wandering through the small town on their way to the next. They were known to be loud. Obnoxious. Always swinging their weapon around to boast about whatever beast or demon they had slain. That was naturally what the people of that small town had come to expect from the barbaric race.

This orc though, was odd. He didn't talk much, nor did he carry a weapon. In fact, the only thing ever seen on his person was an old, raggedy, hardback book. It looked decades old, at the very least. Colors that were once vibrant, now looked worn and washed out. The spine that once held it together sternly, now looked like it could crumble in his hand at any second. The orc kept to himself mostly, as his favorite pastime appeared to be reading that old tome in the library. When he read, his eyes appeared to be glued to every page, mumbling the words to himself as if he was reading through it for the first time. Rarely did he ever talk to anyone unless he was purchasing food or drink.

He slept alone. He had no one that he knew there and took lodge in the only inn available in that small town: Mace and Tulips. A nice little tavern with decent rooms upstairs, though the bar was the main attraction. Full of dancing, singing, good music, and plenty of drinking. It would get rather loud and rowdy at night.

But the orc never participated. Instead, he chose to walk past the dancing people and good drinks to go upstairs and sleep for the night. Everyone wondered why he even stayed. Many expected him to leave after a week—maybe a month at the longest—but he had been here two months now with no signs of departure. Over time, the townspeople grew more and more distant. Their looks sometimes turned to frowns when he passed by. The longer he stayed, the more whispered conversations and gossip emerged. Weeks before he arrived, the town began to have odd occurrences. Travelers and villagers alike were attacked by vicious wildlife and monstrous creatures that hid beneath the darkness of the forest. It was especially terrifying because that small town was surrounded by thick forests on all sides. They were miles away from the next town over, and the citizens were starting to feel panicked and claustrophobic.

Some wanted to blame the orc. Some of them even complained to the mayor that the behemoth should be jailed, hung, or at the very least, exiled. But, the mayor stayed firm that these occurrences happened before the orc arrived, and that he would not kill or send an innocent person out to their death when they had a safe haven here from the vicious monsters. The townspeople had a mixed reaction to his stance, but none protested.

At least, for a while.

However, the decision only made the gray behemoth more of an outcast. Not that he seemed to care all that much. He didn't give a glance at the hushed whispers and odd stares. Even on a night like tonight, when he wasn't in his room, he acted out of place. He sat at a table in the inn by himself while people partied and danced around him. Many fell into a drunken stupor to help take their minds off the impending doom that

PROLOGUE

lurked in the shadows just at the edge of the town.

But he remained one of the very few that night that didn't drink. Instead, he had a glass of water. His usual. No ice. Just... water.

Having someone just sit there reading for hours on end while others danced around him was an odd sight, to say the least. Such an anomaly managed to attract the attention of the bartender from across the room. She leaned over the bar counter with her head resting on her hand, a finger idly tapping her cheek. She wore a white collared button-up shirt with black pants and black suspenders. She had red skin, but her pointy, long ears seemed to indicate that she was an elf.

"It's rude ta stare, lass." A dwarf who was even shorter than the bar counter itself, made his way over. His bald head barely peeked up from behind the bar. There were small ladders and stools here and there so he could climb up and still serve drinks. To get a better view, he pulled one of the small stepping stools closer and stepped up to the bar counter to see what she was looking at. His hand stroked against his long ginger braided beard once he had a good view. "Dat orc again?" the smaller man said.

She frowned at his words, almost cringing at the word 'again'. She responded back, "It's just... what's his deal?" She watched as the orc took a drink of his water and stared at his book. "Who comes to a bar every night just to drink water?" She pursed her lips. "I thought orcs were usually more fun than this."

"Well, *weirdos* tends ta' be in every race." He shrugged his shoulders, but even he had to admit it wasn't the behavior he had seen very often in orcs. "Ah, well. Leave it be, lass. We gots drunks ta' serve." Having thought the conversation was over, he began to climb down the ladder.

But the elf didn't choose to follow his lead. Instead, she pushed off the bar, standing up to her full height. She was fairly tall, standing around six feet at full height. "I'm going over there," she stated bluntly.

"Ugh. I said *leave it be, lass,*" the dwarf waved his hand dismissively.

"Tar's a reason they avoid 'im. Tar be a dark aura comin' from 'im."

"And what do you mean by—" and she gave air quotes for the next part. Clearly she was not taking what he was saying very seriously. "Dark Aura."

"Dark magic, child. Evil. Cursed. Been a while since I seen it, but it takes me back ta' decades ago."

She rolled her eyes and muttered under her breath. "Here we go..."

"Seen it plenty in me youth. Can spot it from a mile away. Ya know I was a cleric fa'—"

"—more than two decades," she said finishing his sentence.

"More than *two decades!*" he said, giving confirmation. "Fought demons, packs o' wolves. Pigmen. Even packs o' wolf demon pigmen."

She let out a sigh. It sounded like he was sprouting his usual tales about the 'grand ol' days' again. She needed to break away before he got too deep into his own nostalgia. "I'm going to go talk to him," the elf said as she moved to grab a large mug from underneath the counter and then started to fill it with some ale from one of the large wooden kegs that were behind them.

The dwarf grimaced, putting his palm to his face. "Ya're as stubborn as a bull, Alyssia."

Now it was her turn to wave dismissively. "Oh, I'm just going to see if he wants some ale, don't make a big deal out of it. Watch the bar for me, Thorne." She swiftly grabbed the handle of the mug and made her way out from behind the bar before she headed over to the lone orc.

Thorne spent a moment watching before muttering to himself, "Please dinna get ya'self in trouble, lass." His gaze grew distracted when he saw a hand go up at the other side of the bar for more ale. "Aye, aye, I'm coming, ya drunkard."

Chapter One

Alyssia made her way over to the hooded orc, ale in hand. Now that she thought about it, the only time she had ever spoken to him before was when she was taking his drink order. Internally she was actually starting to have second thoughts about this. What if Thorne was right? What if he *was* some kind of secret... pigman demon or whatever. She thought about going back, but her pride wouldn't let her return to the bar with her tail between her legs. Even so, her footsteps slowed as she approached him. The orc took notice of her presence quicker than she had anticipated. He raised his gaze from the book that he had been obsessed with, and their eyes made contact. She stood there frozen for a second before the orc himself broke the awkwardness.

"Yes?" His voice sounded tired, rough. A little annoyed even. Almost as if just her invading his space bothered him.

Alyssia was caught off guard. The only words she had heard from him were 'water' or 'just water'. She steeled herself and gave him a smile. "You're the lonely kind of sort, huh?" she said as she put the mug of ale in front of him, which made an audible thud on the table. The hood covered most of his face still, so she had a hard time gauging his emotions.

His hand did not reach for the mug. "I have not requested ale," he said as he took another sip from the glass of water instead.

"S'on the house, actually," Alyssia stated, grabbing a nearby chair and pulling it up to the table where he was sitting. "Mind if I sit down?"

The orc made a sound similar to a low, grumbling hum. From what she could see of his face, he had an annoyed look that seemed to suggest again, that she was interrupting his reading.

Geez, this guy is a hermit, she thought. That was okay, though. She was used to grumpy from dealing with Thorne, so it didn't deter her efforts. "I'll take that as a yes."

She turned the chair around and sat the opposite way so she could rest her arms on the backrest. "I guess you're kind of a cheap skate. I've only ever seen you order water." She pressed, hoping to break the tension with some humor and a smile. The orc did not seem very amused, though. She suspected he did not even know what humor was.

From this angle, she was able to get a better look at him. He had numerous scars spread across his face. There were so many. She tried not to let her expression show her shock at his appearance. Some of the scars could have been from old combat wounds, after all, and she didn't want to come off as rude.

There was a long pause before finally—and carefully—he reached for the mug, grabbing it and bringing it up to his lips to take a large gulp. Half of it went down in almost an instant. "You have my sincerest thanks," he said.

There was a puzzled look on her face before she couldn't help the chuckle that left her. "*Sincerest*? Wow, I think you're the first orc I've ever seen with manners."

"Then you have not seen many orcs." He stated bluntly. The hooded behemoth started to drink the last half of the ale that was in the mug, and her laughter subsided a little sooner than she expected it to.

It was true. Her only interactions with orcs had been the few that traveled through from time to time. She gave a shrug of her shoulders. "Alright. Ya got me there." She said. She watched him down the amount of ale that would have normally taken her half the night and a couple of drunken songs to finish. "I'm Alyssia, by the way," she said.

The large mug came back down to the table empty. "Gorgron," he replied.

She smiled for a moment. Sure, he was a little weird, but he didn't seem harmful. From the corner of her eye, she could tell some of the townspeople were watching them. It was readily apparent to her that she was probably one of the few people to even have been able to hold a conversation with him. Her smile faded just a little when the stares were enough that they even drew the orc's attention. "Oh, don't worry about them," she stated. Then she leaned in a little closer, bringing up her hand to block the movements of her lips from prying eyes. "Between me and you, they freak out over anyone that's not a human, pretty much," she whispered.

"Hmph. Funny." Gorgron said as he simply picked up his book to start reading again.

Alyssia raised her eyebrow and tilted her head curiously. "Hm? What's so funny about it?"

There was just this uncomfortably long pause that followed. And then he closed his book and placed it down. "That an orc makes them uncomfortable... but they allow a demon to serve them liquor."

It would be a lie to say that she wasn't taken aback by his abruptness. Her tone shifted, and her voice raised more than she wanted it to. "*What did you say?*" Then she groaned, "What, have you never seen an elf with red skin before or something?"

"Not ones that frequent this side of the world." He affirmed. His dark eyes peered at her. His expression blank and stare unwavering. It made her uncomfortable. It felt like his eyes were burrowing into her. She felt a chill go down her spine, and she had to wonder if maybe this was why people didn't talk to him.

She tried to shake it off by giving a casual shrug. A weak attempt to hide her uneasiness. "Okay, so you got me again," she relented. "I'm not naturally red. I'm more of a... soft, smokey gray." She was trying to add humor wherever she could in their conversation. It was the only thing keeping her nerves down. She looked down at her red hand. "I was cursed," she said.

Gorgron frowns at that. "Cursed?"

"Yes. By dark magic," she explained. "Happened a *loooong* time ago. Never been able to break it." After saying that, she looked up from her hand and noticed the same stare that he had given her before. Those focused, piercing black eyes were unwavering. There was a long pause of silence between the two that very quickly broke the threshold of how uncomfortable she was willing to be in casual conversation. She stood up, giving an uneasy smile. "Right. Well, uh. I should get back to the bar," she said as she tried to remain cordial as she put the chair back up against the table and picked up the empty mug the orc left. "Hope you enjoyed the free ale!" Alyssia didn't say anything else. She just made her way over to the bar, almost speed-walking back.

By the time she arrived behind the bar counter again, her expression was a lot less excited than it was when she had first left.

Thorne noticed immediately. To avoid any eavesdropping, he got close and whispered to her. "Is everything alright, lass? What did he say ta ya?" There was obvious concern in his voice but also a mixture of building anger.

She knew Thorne. If she said the wrong thing here, the next thing that would happen was a blunderbuss being shoved up the orc's nose. She gave him a smile and placed a hand on his shoulder.

"I'm fine, Thorne," she said as she glanced over her shoulder at Gorgron. He had gone back to reading his book. "He was... surprisingly polite, I guess...?" she said.

Thorne's eyebrow raised with a curious look. As if a comment on his mannerisms was the last thing he expected to hear. She turns her gaze back to Thorne before speaking again, "I don't think he's some devout saint, but... I just don't feel like he's the reason the monsters are here, you know?"

CHAPTER ONE

Thorne crossed his arms and gave a nod in agreement. "Aye, lass. Tha' I alreadae knew. The monsters were spotted weeks before he arrived." He gave a shake of his head. "Blame is bein' thrown his way because he was one o' the last travelers ta arrive before the beasts became too dangerous fa' us ta leave." Thorne said, confirming her gut instincts.

Alyssia didn't say anything for a moment. But then she grabbed some mugs so she could start taking orders again. "Come on, Thorne. Still got thirsty, drunk customers to serve, right?"

Thorne just gave a laugh. "Aye, lass. Aye."

The rest of the night was about as uneventful as it always was. Drunk guys tossed a few flirts Alyssia's way, a couple fights had to be broken up. Nothing out of the ordinary for the inn. Once things had slowed down, Thorne let Alyssia have the rest of the night off, saying that he would finish closing down the bar himself. The amazing part that she liked about working here was that after work, she could go right up to her room and go to sleep. Thorne gave her room and board as a perk, but of course, he docked her pay every month for it. He wasn't exactly known for being charitable.

She went through her normal nightly routine before slipping into bed, the mattress creaking in protest as she got under the covers and laid down for the night. Normally she went to sleep fairly quickly. A night of running back and forth and breaking up bar fights was enough to put her out the moment her head hit the pillow. But tonight, her mind wandered. She found herself tossing and turning, unable to fully find rest. Eventually, she got annoyed enough that she temporarily gave up on the idea of sleeping for the night. She sat up in her bed in a basic white nightgown, running her fingers through her hair and scratching at her scalp. From all the tossing and turning, she was sure she had one of the worst cases of bedhead ever seen.

She didn't feel inclined to fix it. Instead, she groaned as she moved out of bed, begrudgingly. She decided that going on a walk might help clear her head a bit. She left her room and explored the inn, the silence of the night only being interrupted by the light creaking of the floorboards as the red-tinted elf made her way toward the stairs to go back down to the bar. She noticed that as she got closer, she could hear the faint sound of banging noises that only seemed to get louder as she ventured closer.

She spotted Thorne with some planks of wood, a hammer, and some nails. He was boarding up the front entrance and the windows. She arched an eyebrow as she witnessed the strange sight. "Uuuh. Thorne?" she asked curiously as she approached.

"Up late, aren'tcha, lass?" the dwarf acknowledged her in a friendly tone, but did not stop what he was doing. He held up another nail and started to hammer it into a plank of wood over the window. There was a moment of pause from her. It was far too late at night for her to want to deal with Thorne's shenanigans, but she decided to ask anyway. She stepped closer, leaning forward to peek over the dwarf's shoulder. "Thorne... what are you doing?" she asked in a curious tone.

"Boardin' up the windows, lass. Just in case a monster decides ta stroll inta town, we'll be readae." About a month or so ago, Alyssia would have thought he was being paranoid. But, with everything going on... she could actually appreciate the sentiment. He was very thorough when it came to his guests' safety. There was just one thing that bothered her about the whole idea. "Thorne, how is anyone supposed to leave tonight? What if someone wants some fresh air?"

"Waitin' till morning fa' some fresh air ain't gonna kill 'em." The dwarf grumbled and grabbed another nail before proceeding to hammer it into the wooden plank, just like he did the last one.

Wrinkles formed on her forehead, and she pinched hard at the bridge of her nose in annoyance. "Okay. Then look, *I'm* going to get some fresh air before I'm sealed in for the night," she said. She swore that talking to

Thorne was like talking to a brick wall sometimes.

The dwarf gave a nod. "Suit ya'self, lass. Just make sure ya're back in thortae. Once I board up the doors, thar's no one in or out."

She rolled her eyes, and made her way over to the door, grabbing the knob. "Don't worry. I'll be back in 'thortae'." She said, mocking the way he said the word 'thirty'. With a swing of the door, she made her way outside. She loved the calm and peacefulness that night brought. She adored the small town of Green Haven during the day, but there was a certain stillness that could only be felt when the hustle and bustle of the day was at its end.

Everything felt at peace. Silent. She was even still barefoot, she realized. The cold touch of the paved, stone streets, gave a welcomed sensation underneath her.

She smiled as she ventured through the town, aiming for nowhere in particular. It was a relatively simple place. The vast majority of the houses were basic timber-framed builds. There were a few of them here and there that were made from brick, but she enjoyed the simple look and feel of it all. It felt... homely. It was a far cry from the extravagance she grew up around as an elf child, but this all felt different. Like she belonged here. She hummed a tune, the sound of her voice being the only one that was present throughout the streets. She became lost in thought the more she wandered.

As she looked around, she noticed more and more that Thorne wasn't the only one that was starting to board up his windows now. It wasn't all the houses, but it was enough to take notice of. This was such a peaceful town. She just couldn't grasp why these monsters were so fixated on them. By the time she snapped out of her trance-like state, she had found herself at the very edge of the town near the forest. There was a large meadow with a paved road that led straight to it. It was strange to think about now, but kids used to play here. In fact, often times she would come out here in the afternoon just to watch the children play. Hearing the sounds of their laughter and how much fun they were having always brought a smile to her face. It reminded her of when she was their age.

To the far right of the meadow was a monument that was Green Haven's staple and main tourist attraction. A giant axe that was blade first into the dirt with its handle tilted upward. Now centuries old by this point, the axe was heavily rusted, but it marked the burial ground of Bhrog the Gargantuan. He was said to have been the largest and most ruthless cyclops to have ever lived. He had grown to be literally the size of a small mountain. Legends had said it took his cyclops brethren days to dig up a hole that was big enough to bury him.

She wasn't exactly a history buff, but there were quite a few people in town that had talked her ear off about it. To the point that now she was able to recite several old legends about him at the bar to travelers. She didn't believe half of them, but it normally brought her some good tips.

She sighed at the thought, though. Travelers and wandering merchants were practically nonexistent these days. Not wanting to depress herself any further, she turned around, deciding to head back into town. She had lost track of time, and the last thing she needed was for Thorne to be finished and for her to be stuck sleeping on the street until sunrise. Besides, her eyelids were beginning to feel heavy again. This time she would have a much better chance of a good night's sleep.

But, as she went to leave, she heard... faint whispers that pierced through the silence of the night air. They were so faint that the light breeze of the wind and ruffle of the bushes had shielded the sound before, but now she heard it more clearly. She looked around but didn't see anything in her immediate vicinity. Throughout the meadow, there were these large shrubs that the kids often used for their hide-and-seek games. They made it nearly impossible to see fully into the meadow just by looking at it.

She bit her lip at the thought of just returning to town and forgetting she had ever heard it. But the sound was alluring, and it sparked her curiosity. *Alyssia, you're an idiot,* she thought to herself before cautiously making her way deeper into the meadow, inevitably wandering closer to the dark forest that was just up ahead. Her pupils enlarged, adjusting to the darkness that was slowly engulfing her as she moved further away from the faint glow of the torches in town. A fair amount of her sight relied on just the moonlight. But being an elf did have its perks. She wasn't an owl, but she could see a little better in the dark than say, a human.

The whispering became louder and louder. Her heart was beating through her chest while she weaved through the shrubs. Finally, she happened to peer around the right bunch of shrubbery and quickly covered her mouth to keep from gasping. It was Gorgron. He was on his knees with his back to her, around five yards away. His robe was discarded next to him, which left the gray-colored orc fully unclothed. His back and what she could see of his arms were all littered with scars. Some new, some old. Some looked somewhere in between. His body almost looked like some kind of map. It was unlike anything she had seen before.

She watched as he whispered in some language she didn't understand and saw him bow his head over and over again at nothing. It was like he was worshipping something. Every race had some type of god they prayed to, but never had she seen an orc do this. Most of their gods strived for carnage and combat. Not peaceful worshipping ceremonies.

After he bowed a few more times, the orc brought up his empty right hand, palm facing upward. With his left, he picked up a small knife and proceeded to lay the sharp edge of the blade into his palm. It made her feel nauseous seeing the blade cutting deep into the flesh of his palm. He let his blood drip down onto the ground, staining the grass below as he seemed to lift his hands in prayer. He then bowed forward with his arms stretched.

Alyssia was frozen. She knew next to nothing about the use of dark magic, but it didn't take an expert to figure out this was some kind of ritual. Thorne had been right in telling her to stay away from him. She should have listened. She was kicking herself for even coming out here so late. Cautiously, she started to back up to leave. She had hoped his prayers would keep him occupied long enough that he wouldn't take notice of her. Instead, his prayers seemed to come to an end abruptly. She couldn't see his face, but she could tell that he had snapped out of whatever hypnotic state of mind he had been in when she got there.

Gorgron's body appeared to stiffen and shift, and her heart almost stopped when she saw his head gradually turn toward her. When she looked into his eyes, there was nothing there. Just two empty cavities that once held them. It was like they had been ripped out.

There was a long moment of pause. Even though he shouldn't have been able to see, it felt to her like he knew exactly where she was. No words were exchanged between them. The orc simply groaned and then proceeded to turn away from her again.

She didn't waste any time after that. She quickly turned around and sprinted back toward the town. She didn't stop for anything, not even to breathe. Loud, quickened footsteps echoed throughout the stone-paved streets, only coming to a stop when she had made her way all the way back to the inn. Out of breath and breathing heavily, she took a moment to rest in front of Mace and Tulips' large double doors. Adrenaline still filled her veins, and her heart was beating so fast she could hear it through her ears.

Not long after she was there, Thorne opened the door. He was still waiting on Alyssia to get back when he heard her panting for breath just outside. "Lass! What's wrong?" He asked, sounding worried.

There was a pause from her as she didn't say anything at first. Partly because her breath hadn't fully come back. After a few seconds of filling her lungs, she finally responded. "I'm— I'm fine. Is everything almost boarded up?"

Thorne looked confused. "Aye, lass. Couple boards and nails should do the trick. But— lass. Are ya sure ya're alright—"

"Fine, Thorne. Just—get it boarded up, okay? Please?" She walked past him and started to head upstairs to her room again, holding her head which was now throbbing. She let out a sigh of relief that she had made it back safely.

The dwarf looked puzzled at her strange behavior. He knew something odd was going on, but didn't want to pry too much on the subject. He picked up one of the few boards that was left for the final door and started to hammer. Before she disappeared out of sight upstairs, he did ask a question though; "Did ya see any stragglers from the inn tha' hadn't come back yet?"

She stopped on the stairs as soon as she heard his question. After a pause, she gave a shake of her head. "Nope... no one." She said. And then she proceeded to head upstairs for the night. That was all the confirmation that he needed as he boarded up the final door.

Unsurprisingly, Alyssia went to her bed feeling just as uncomfortable as she did the first time around. But, eventually, the day caught up to her, and her eyes practically closed on their own. The thought of Thorne still being up helped her to relax as well. She knew *no one* was getting in with the way he was going to board the place up. Despite the odd night she had just experienced, she found herself snoring before long.

Her falling asleep happened so subtly that she barely remembered doing it. Only waking up the next morning from the sun hitting her face through the window. She felt groggy, stiff, and a little sore from the hard sprint she had done the previous night. She let out a groan as she sat up in her bed, the sunlight peeking in through her curtains as the day was getting started. Her head was swimming with thoughts. She wasn't sure exactly what she had witnessed that night. What was Gorgron's deal? Was he evil or some kind of demon in disguise? Why hadn't he just attacked her when she was alone? So many questions she had.

The creaking sounds of the floorboards were becoming more constant outside her door as more people were beginning to start their day. Luckily, this was her day off. If it wasn't, Thorne would have been calling her down to help with the bar. Very few people consumed alcohol this early in the morning, but as he always said, 'it's never ta' earlae fa' a drink'. Spoken like a true dwarf. No wonder the only food they served was nuts and berries.

Under any normal circumstances, she would have gone back to sleep, but as things were, she got her day started. She went through her typical morning routine before throwing on a shirt and some pants. She made her way downstairs and headed immediately for the door. By the time she got her hand on the doorknob, she could hear Thorne's voice from the bar.

"'Ey, lass!" he yelled out. She turned around, seeing him at the bar and serving a crowd of people drinks already. She really wished he would stop serving people drinks first thing in the morning. She doubted any of them had eaten breakfast yet. "Everything alright?" The dwarf said, pouring a mug of ale for a customer.

Alyssa nodded her head and looked at him with a confident smile. He was never going to let it go unless she showed him she was okay in some way or another. "Just getting some fresh air, Thorne. Be back soon!" She gave him a wave and with that, she walked out of the inn and started to make her way through town. She wasn't able to stop the feeling of constant unease. She was always looking over her shoulder or down any dark area or alley. No hooded orc was anywhere in sight, though.

She headed to the town's local potion shop. It was a small store. Kind of cute, really. In this town, potions were an incredibly niche attraction. Most people in Green Haven preferred to do things by hand. But, of course, travelers enjoyed them. There was also the occasional odd potion or knick-knack that would come in handy from time to time.

CHAPTER ONE

She opened the door to the shop, causing the little bell that was overhead to ring and alert the owner she was there. The place had an old, dusty smell. This was originally an old bookstore before the place changed owners. The smell seemed almost as if it was ingrained into the very walls of the establishment itself. There were wooden bookshelves filled with different colors of potions with little tags on them to indicate their price.

She approached the wooden storefront counter when the owner suddenly emerged from the back of the shop carrying an arm full of potions and papers. He had on a simple beige-colored robe that was just a shade or two lighter than his skin. His glasses were practically hanging off his face. He had clearly come to the front in a rush, with the possibility of a new customer filling him with excitement. "Welcome! Welcome to Magic Trinkets—" he stopped himself mid-sentence before he could completely finish it. Seeing Alyssia made his excited smile fade to a dull and bored look. "Oh. Alyssia, it's just you," he said in a bland tone.

She could feel her eye twitch. "*Just me*? Wow, Pin, save your enthusiasm," she huffed.

He let out a sigh as he sat his items down on the counter, letting them tumble together in a mess he would sort out later. "I'm sorry, it's just... well, you know business has been slow lately. I haven't had a new customer in weeks. Only the regulars." Pin's words carried with them a rather defeated tone that made Alyssia's expression soften.

She remembered when he first came into town around a year ago and how excited he was to start his business. He's young, practically still a kid in her eyes. She had her doubts that a potion shop would work in a simple town like this, but she had hoped the best for him. It made her sad that it wasn't working out due to the lack of travelers coming through. The boy was really wasting his talents here anyway. Someone smart enough to craft their own elixirs from scratch should be in one of the big cities, not a simple town like this. She put on a smile. "Have you tried advertising?

Maybe put up some flyers around town? I'm surprised people haven't been flocking here in droves with everything going on," she said.

He shook his head, taking the time to adjust his glasses back to their original position. "You would think so. But most people here are stubborn. They don't really trust it." He took a moment and looked down at the number of potions in front of him. So much time and effort he had put into these just so they could sit on store shelves.

"Don't trust it?" Alyssia chuckled. "That's silly. What, they think they're going to blow up if they drink one or something?"

Her words caused Pin's expression to brighten immediately. "That's what I've been telling them! Only *some of the potions* will make you blow up. And that's only if you don't follow the instructions! Why is that so hard for people to understand?"

Alyssia's laughter soon started to fade as her expression became more uneasy. "Right. Yeah. Hey... So, Pin? Maybe just don't mention the blowing-up part right out of the gate? Not really a good conversation starter, you know?"

Pin sighed and moved to sit down in a chair that was behind the counter, feeling defeated. "I guess." He placed his elbow on the counter and rested his head in his palm. "Too bad I didn't decide to become a gunsmith... or a blacksmith. Those guys are making a killing around town right now," he said.

It was true. Alyssia had seen long lines of people trying to buy any kind of weapon or armor they could get their hands on. The gun makers and blacksmiths were working around the clock just to meet the new demand. She looked down at the assortment of potions that were on the table and picked up one with pink liquid in a glass vial. "Well, luckily for you, I'm an elf. And I'm not afraid of a little magic." She swished the liquid around inside the vial. "And I need to protect myself too. So, what does this one do?"

"It allows you to breath fire."

She quickly put the vial back down on the table. "Okaaay. A little much for my tastes." She pointed to a blue vial, taping her finger on it. "And this one?"

"Ah! That one lets you shoot a bolt of lightning from your eyes," Pin responded.

Her face visibly cringed. She grabbed another one. "This one?"

"Oh no, not that one! Mages use it for combat, but if you don't know what you're doing, your organs will spill out of your—"

"Whoa, whoa, whoa!" Alyssia interrupted. "Hey, look. Let's switch gears. I'm going to be *reeeal* specific." After talking to him, she was starting to understand why he wasn't selling much. "I just want to be able to punch someone in the face really hard if I need to. You got anything for that?"

Pin gave a hum as he thought about it for a second. Then he got up and walked to the other side of the store, rubbing his chin while he looked at the assortment of potions on the shelf. He had his eye on one in particular. He grabbed a vial full of yellow liquid and walked back over to the counter. He sat it down in front of her. "This will do it. If you drink this, you will gain the strength of a cyclops."

Alyssia picked it up, her eyes beaming. "Seriously!? You're telling me I'll have the strength of Bhrog?" she asked as she flexed her biceps barbarically. "Me Bhrog! Bhrog strong! Bhrog mighty!" She grinned.

"A *regular* cyclops," Pin corrected.

"Oh," Alyssia said, the revelation killing her enthusiasm.

"Are you sure you don't want something that's more effective in a self-defense scenario? Maybe stone skin? Or porcupine quills?" As he spoke, Pin held up each vial, swishing around their contents enticingly. He seemed a little *too* excited about the effects of these potions.

She winced a little at the thought of growing porcupine quills. "I... appreciate it. But I think I'll skip that. I have a thing about making potential permanent alterations to my body," she said.

"But they're not permanent. The potions only have a temporary effect."

"I know, I know. It's not you, I promise. It's just— I don't care for it." Her tone and visual appearance appeared to shift at the subject.

Not one to pry, Pin nodded his head and adjusted his glasses. "Fair enough."

She grabbed the potion and pocketed it before she placed some silver coins on the table. "Hopefully, this is enough to cover it. Keep the change."

He smiled and picked up the silver she put down. It had only cost two silver, and she had given him five. He could appreciate the tip. "Thanks. Times are... a bit rough right now," he admitted.

"Don't sweat it. Thanks for the help."

At that point, she could hear a couple dozen or so footsteps passing by the shop. Alyssia turned around and saw a large number of townsfolk that all appeared to be heading in one direction. Presumably, where the town square was.

She raised an eyebrow. "Did I miss something? What's going on?"

"You didn't know?" Pin asked, starting to take the potions on the counter and put them up on the shelves. "The mayor called a meeting for the town. He's going to discuss the monsters and what we're going to do about them."

Her memory flooded back about the occasion. "Oh, shoot, that's today!? It must've slipped my mind." She headed toward the open door but stopped by the time she reached the door frame as she noticed Pin wasn't following her. "Aren't you coming?"

When she asked this, she noticed his expression and mood seemed to plummet. He looked to have become a little depressed, even.

"Yeah. I'll uh... I'll follow behind later." Pin said, continuing to put several of the items away.

"Sure... See you there." She wondered why he was acting so odd, but she didn't have time to dwell. She left the store, leaving Pin alone as she went out onto the streets to follow the large gathering of people to the center of town.

In the town square, there was a wooden, raised platform with a podium. Just about every person in town was here, and worse of all, she was all the way in the back. She tried to tip-toe to get a better view, and that's when she spotted the mayor stepping up onto the platform. Despite her placement in the crowd, she could just make out the bags under his eyes from an obvious lack of sleep. It was apparent that the rising number of reports of citizens being butchered by monstrous creatures was taking its toll.

She swore it looked like he'd aged ten years in the last two months. The bags under his eyes, a few grays here and there sprouting from the roots of his braided locks. He had seen better days. Behind him was the captain of the town guard, sporting his full silver knight armor. He left his helmet off, showing the crowd his bright blond hair and mustache. The mayor walked over to the podium and seemed to steel himself for a brief moment before he took a deep breath and announced to the crowd with a loud, booming voice. "Citizens of Green Haven!"

And almost immediately, as if on cue, said citizens all started to roar in anger and frustration. Clearly, they weren't happy and were eager to voice their concerns.

"What are you going to do about this!?"

"I'm afraid to even have my kids go outside!"

"Why can't the guards stop these monsters!?"

The mayor raised his hands in surrender to calm them down. "Citizens, we are doing the best we can—"

"Your best hasn't been good enough!" an angry man roared from the crowd.

"I know. It has not been. This is why I wanted to make this announcement. In five days time, we will be taking the fight to them. I will be taking half of the town's guards south through the forest to the capital of Westvale. From there, we can request aid and finally end this horrific nightmare."

There was a mixed reaction about the plan from the crowd. Some cheered that they were finally getting back at those vile creatures, but some townsfolk looked a little nervous. Perhaps they were the husbands and wives of those in the guards that were about to get sent off to what could be their deaths.

Alyssia herself wasn't so sure about the plan. She chewed on her lower lip. Was the blunt force method really the best idea? It wasn't like she had any bright ideas either. They had tried to send messages by doves weeks ago to no avail. Scouts would disappear into the forest to never return again. And with how simple the town was, there was no magical means of communication. She just wasn't sure that the town's guards were strong enough to survive whatever those creatures were.

The rest of what the mayor was saying was starting to blend into the background of her own thoughts. It was just a lot of political jargon to try and calm the people's nerves and put them at ease. However, out of the corner of her eye, she could see a large hooded figure moving away from the crowd. Without a doubt, it was Gorgron. He couldn't exactly blend in with a crowd made up of mostly humans.

She thought about ignoring him, but she just had to know for sure he wasn't the one causing the destruction to this town. What was he even doing last night? She reached into her pocket where she had put the vial of Cyclops Strength. It gave her a sense of security, knowing it was within reach whenever she needed it.

She navigated through the crowd, moving swiftly in the orc's general direction as he went down the now empty streets of Green Haven. She masked her presence the best she could. Whenever he turned a corner or went down an alleyway, she waited a minute before trailing behind him. It wasn't like he was easy to miss. Even when the streets were full, you could spot an orc in this town. But the more she followed him, the more she noticed his strange behavior. She saw him bend down occasionally and slide his index and middle finger along the stone road before rubbing any dirt he had collected between his fingertips. He looked to be wandering around aimlessly, but there was an obvious intent to his actions. He examined the houses, the ground, the walls. All in the same manner. It was a strange sight, to say the least.

What was he looking for? It was like he was investigating something. She spotted the orc going down another alleyway and waited a minute before following him. However, the moment she did, she jumped—almost shrieked—in surprise and stumbled back, nearly falling over. Standing right there in the alley, was Gorgron. Peering at her with a dull expression. She could feel her heart racing through her chest as she started to fumble in her pocket for the vial of Cyclops Strength.

"You've been following me," the orc said in a matter-of-fact tone. Almost as if he talked about the weather. He didn't appear to make any moves that showed hostility. Just stood there, watching her.

By this point, she had the potion out and firmly in her grasp. She narrowed her eyes. "Who... *are* you?" The words left her lips before she could really process what she was trying to say.

"I've told you my name." his voice sounded low and deep with a hint of frustration. Alyssia frowned and took a step forward. "Hey. Cut the bull, okay? I saw you in the meadow. I don't know what the hell you were chanting about, but it—" She paused for a moment and kept her hand clutched around the vial. "—it was like you were... worshipping." Just saying the word 'worshipping' caused her to shutter as if she was defiling the word by even calling it that.

Gorgron didn't deny it. In fact, he didn't say anything at first. But eventually, he would grab the edges of his hood and then pull it back, fully revealing his face. The deep scars were even more apparent in the daylight, clearly as scarred as the rest of his body. His eyes had returned to normal as well.

"Because I was."

His answer just brought about more questions than answers. "Why would you need to *cut* yourself in order to worship? Are you some kind of... cultist!?" she asked, her voice raising in volume due to frustration.

"Cultist!? No, no. Gods, no." It was as if he was taken aback by just the idea of being called that. "I am but a simple and humble servant of The Wise One."

When he said this, Alyssia wondered if she was being tricked. She had half expected him to threaten or try to kill her, not to spark up a conversation. "The Wise One?" she asked with a wrinkle of her nose and the raise of an eyebrow. Was that some kind of deity? There seemed to be so many these days that she could hardly keep track.

At her question, Gorgron appeared to take on a brighter demeanor for the first time. He had an awful fanged smile that crept up upon his features as if just talking about this supposedly higher being was enough to fill him with joy and break him out of his shell.

"Yes. Yes, The Wise One," the orc said as he crept closer, his twisted smile making her stomach tighten into a knot. "He is the ruler of all! The Ultimate Being!"

His voice got louder, and her eyes darted around to see if anyone else was nearby. But the streets were empty. He took another big step, almost closing the gap between them. It forced her to take a few steps back in response.

"He is the savior and salvation of everything and nothing. We live only by his grace!"

"Don't take another step, you psycho!" Alyssia yelled. She popped the cork of the vial in her hand and brought it up to her lips. She was just moments away from drinking it but stopped when she noticed that Gorgron hadn't taken another step. He'd respected her wishes and chose to just stand there.

He looked almost disappointed. As if he was expecting something different out of her response. Did he really think she was going to listen to his little sermon on some god she had never heard of? For a very brief moment, she felt a twinge of pity for him.

He spoke again. "I misjudged you. You are not ready to receive his blessings." That was all he said before he put his hood back on and proceeded to walk away.

She was left confused and disoriented. After all of that, she was *still* uncertain of just who he was. These were some of the oddest interactions she'd ever had, and while she felt uneasy, it didn't seem like his intent was to harm her. He could have done so a few times over by now.

She mused in her head about what she should do as a few seconds of time passed. She ultimately said a curse under her breath, put the cork back on the vial, and tucked it into her pocket. She figured she would regret it, but she walked quickly toward the orc, deciding to follow behind him again. He was not fast or mysterious. He didn't vanish when he turned the corner, nor did he do anything mythical. He was just walking at a normal speed and doing the same thing as before. She moved closer to him cautiously. She had to know. "What are you doing...? What are you looking for?"

He didn't seem as annoyed by her presence as he had before. He was focused on his task. He kneeled down on one knee and pulled up some of the grass that had grown through the cracks in the stone before letting it fall back to the ground. "I am looking for guidance," he said bluntly as he rose back to full height. "I am hoping The Wise One will lead me."

She looked confused again. "Lead you to what?"

The orc didn't answer right away, giving a low hum instead while he looked around the immediate area with purpose. "There is something happening to this town. But I cannot pin point what."

If this was a less serious conversation, she would have sarcastically gasped. It didn't take a psychic to know that the town was in dire straits.

As it stood now, she just gave him an annoyed look with pursed lips. "Wow, nothing gets past you, Gorgron,"

Alyssia was feeling a headache starting to form. She closed her eyes and began to massage her temple. By the time she opened her eyes again, she saw that the orc had already walked away. Being determined to find answers, she decided to continue to follow him as he moved.

When Gorgron spoke again, it sounded more like he was thinking out loud. "The amount of beasts being attracted to this town feels... unnatural. Artificial." As he examined certain things, it was almost as if he were looking with a different set of eyes than she was. She wondered if he was looking for traces of magic. Even as an elf, she had to admit she had never tried doing such things before, but she had heard tales of such abilities being possible from other elves and from Thorne.

Or maybe she was giving him far too much credit. There was a good chance he was just a crazed lunatic. Well, okay, he *was* a crazed lunatic. But if what he was saying was true, that just made their current situation all the worse. She followed him around for at least half an hour, watching as he repeated much of the same actions he did before over and over again. Rubbing his fingers across surfaces or picking up random bits of dirt and grass. It was all... incredibly boring. But there was a question floating around in her head. "Gorgron. Just curious. How do you know all of this for sure?"

"Because The Wise One has revealed these things to me," Gorgron said this with such absolute certainty; it was as if it was the clearest thing in the world.

Yeah. He was definitely a lunatic. And honestly, she regretted wasting her time—watching him rub at the ground and pat at buildings. She sighed. It was her one day off, and she hadn't even gotten to enjoy it. She resolved that she was going to go back to the inn to take a much-deserved middle-of-the-day nap.

She turned to leave him to his business but found herself stopping suddenly. It was faint, but she could hear the sounds of kids playing nearby. She hadn't fully realized just how close they were to the edge of town, near the meadows. She took a moment to walk toward the sound of the children's laughter and smiled when she spotted them playing hide-and-seek out in the meadow. Obviously, they weren't supposed to be so close to the forest. They must have snuck out of the house or away from their parents to do so. With most of the town being at the meeting, it was no surprise that some kids were able to sneak away unnoticed.

It was nice seeing and hearing them play again. It was only now that she herself had realized just how much was being taken away from the youth of this town. By this point, they were being forced to stay indoors or monitored by their parents around the clock. Gorgron, as crazy as he was, seemed to be the only one who even had a clue about what was going on. Should she side with the desperate mayor or trust the lunatic cultist? Feeling unsure, she stared off into the distance for a minute or so before Gorgron joined her in watching over the children. Alyssia shook her head. "I just want things to return to how they were before."

Gorgron remained stoic for a while. But eventually, his gaze shifted from the children to her. "Change will only come with sacrifice. You cannot be passive."

She dwelled on his words for a moment. Even if he was a lunatic, he did have a point. She just wasn't sure how she was going to help stop all of this.

But, she would worry about that later. It was nice seeing the kids play, but she couldn't in good conscious let them keep going. It was still dangerous out here, after all. She walked out into the meadow, calling to them. "Alright, guys! I know you want to play, but I have to be the boring adult now and—"

It was just then that there was a sudden piercing scream coming from a few of the kids who were out of sight. Instinctually, her body moved before her mind did. She wasn't the fastest, but she could sprint when she needed to. It sent chills down her spine as she pictured every terrible scenario possible. But nothing mentally could have prepared her for the source of the children's screams.

In front of her stood a large demonic beast. A dark-furred wolf-like creature on all fours with glowing yellow eyes that bulged from their sockets. Its jaw was large enough that she swore it could have bitten her in half with one bite if it wanted to, and deep in those powerful jaws was the limp body of a small boy. She vaguely recognized him. He was the baker's son, she believed. The other kids were crying and screaming. They were just as paralyzed in fear as she was. Time around them appeared to stand still, but the creature was still moving. The monster tossed the boy's body to the side as if it had no more use to the creature. Then, it set its sights on the other children. Its yellow eyes appeared to literally roll and rotate in different directions like a chameleon's would. Fresh blood was still dripping from the beast's jaws from its last victim, staining the green grass below it.

Alyssia did her best to will herself to move, but her body never did. The sight of what she had just witnessed was so jarring, so unexpected, and so sudden that she was still in mental disarray. The potion in her pocket didn't even cross her mind. In her head, everything played out in slow motion. The hideous creature positioned its hind legs and angled itself forward to pounce on another child. Mere seconds to act felt like an eternity to her, but she couldn't do anything.

Thankfully, Gorgron didn't share her same issue with inactivity. He sprung into action immediately, rushing past her and getting in front of the little girl the beast had its eyes on just as it attacked. Not caring to be contested, the creature opened its mouth wider in response to its new target. It's jaw almost looked to become freakishly unhinged with full intent to bite off the orc's head along with part of his torso.

Instead, the orc shoved his fist into the beast's mouth, causing it to bite down instinctively and prematurely on the orc's arm. If he were a human or an elf, his arm would have been ripped out of its socket, but thanks to the orcs' natural thick bone density and condensed muscle, the wolf wasn't able to tear through his arm on the first bite. Although blood was drawn, he faired far better from the attack than most other races would have.

The feral creature was large enough that it could fit the orc's entire arm into its mouth all the way up to his shoulder, where the beast's front teeth had sunk. It was at this time that Alyssia finally snapped out of her trance and finally remembered the Cyclops' Strength potion. "G-Gorgron, hold on, I'm coming—" Before Alyssia could even finish her sentence, she saw the feral beast's body start to tremble uncontrollably where it stood. It let out loud, screeching whines that almost caused the elf to cover her ears. The only reason she didn't was because she had chosen to cover her mouth instead.

First, the monster's fur began to fall from its body as smooth and simple as easing off a fur coat. Large piles of now-dead fur covered the grass below. Then, its skin almost seemed to cook from the inside; the flesh started to bubble. The creature's cries slowly subsided as it was undone before her very eyes.

The monster's steaming flesh gradually became liquefied and started to ooze off of its own skeleton. Skin, muscles, and organs all dripped off of its frame and became nothing more than a foul-smelling puddle on the ground. She couldn't recall clearly at what stage the demonic creature's cries had ceased, but it was clear that there was no life left in it. Without muscle to hold it up, the skeleton just flopped over harmlessly to the ground. A pile of useless bones that lay atop a puddle of its own biology.

By this point, the children had scattered, running back to the town to inevitably tell their parents about what had just occurred. Alyssia wasn't sure if she should be horrified by what she had just witnessed or content that at least one of those monsters would never hurt another child again. Her stomach had its own opinions on the matter, though. She found herself hunched over before proceeding to empty what little was in her stomach onto the grassy fields.

It was only now that she remembered that she had skipped breakfast.

Chapter Two

"This is not going to go well," Gorgron mused as he followed behind Alyssia. They had been invited to go see the mayor to discuss the incident that occurred the day before.

"We have to *make* it go well," Alyssia stated as her footsteps came to a halt. She took a moment to look at the orc with a worried expression. She hoped it would convey to him just how important this was for the town. "These people are *dying*, Gorgron. And if this town can use your magic to save lives, then… it's worth it."

Gorgron didn't respond right away. Instead, he chose to pause for a few seconds, followed by a low hum of thought. "Hmm. I thought my magic disturbed you," he said.

Then it was Alyssia's turn to pause. By this point, they had arrived at Green Haven's town hall. It was a modest size. Not as massive or encompassing as the ones in the larger cities, but it was fitting for a smaller town like this.

"I'm not going to lie. It does. A lot," Alyssia admitted as she knocked on the town hall's doors. "But if it's that or letting more kids die, then… I choose your magic."

It wasn't long before she received an answer to the knock. Opening the town hall's door was Eldridge, the leader of the guardsmen. He was clad in full knight armor but wasn't so rude as to have his helmet on. But still, the sight of seeing him in full armor, even for a meeting like this, made Alyssia wonder if he'd slept in it. It was strange to think that just around two months ago, the guardsmen hardly ever had a need to even wear their armor. And now, they seemed to all wear it around the clock.

Eldridge regarded the two with a smile. "Ah, Alyssia," he said as he then turned his gaze to the orc. "And Gorgron, was it?"

Gorgron simply regarded him and gave a nod in response.

Alyssia spoke again, "Eldridge, hi. The mayor sent word that he wanted to see us?"

The guardsman did not hesitate to open the doors wider and took a step aside to allow them to come in. "Yes. Yes, of course. Please, come in."

Once they were inside, Eldridge closed the door behind them. "Please, this way." he proceeded to escort them directly toward the mayor's office. When one thought of what a town hall might look like, cozy was probably near the bottom of the list. But this one was. There were numerous windows and some rooms, but there was nothing that screamed fancy about the interior. When people came by to talk to him, he didn't want them to feel nervous or uneasy, and it worked. Alyssia immediately felt more comfortable. It felt like walking into a friend's house.

"On behalf of the town, I wanted to say thank you, Gorgron. Without your assistance, who knows what would have happened to those children," Eldridge said, taking a glance back at the orc and noticing his arm wrapped in bandages from the shoulder all the way down to his hand. The sleeve of his robe had been torn off from the beast as well. He had to admire the resilience of orcs. A normal man would probably be in so much pain he could hardly get out of bed, and yet this orc was walking around like normal. "We should also get a tailor to take a look at your clothes. It's the least we could do."

Gorgron shook his head in response. "There is no need. The Wise One will provide." Gorgron spoke in this blunt and assumptive manner as if the deity's presence was absolute. It left Eldridge looking confused. Alyssia, not wanting to ruin their chances, decided to intervene. "Gorgron is a very, uh—*religious* man," Alyssia stumbled over her words as she tried to come up with an excuse to hide just how crazy the orc actually was. "He sees trials and tribulations as a test of his faith," she said.

At the very least it worked, as Eldridge nodded to her. "Ah. I see. Well, if The Wise One was to ever permit it, we would be more than happy to help."

Alyssia let out a sigh of relief. This was going to be much harder than she had anticipated. Soon the trio arrives at the mayor's door, and Eldridge— keeping with his mannerisms—gave a few light knocks on the door. He only opened it after the mayor said to come in.

Once they entered, they could see the mayor sitting in his chair, reading over some papers. He looked up when they walked in, and while he tried to brighten his expression with a smile, he simply looked drained and tired. Even here in his office, he wore a simple set of leather armor. It was obvious that the entire town was on high alert. "Gorgron, Alyssia. Please, come in. Have a seat." He gestured to the two chairs on the other side of his desk. "Gorgron, I want to start by saying that you have our town's utmost gratitude for what you did yesterday. We cannot thank you enough for protecting the children."

Gorgron only gave a hum of approval in response as he proceeded to have a seat in the chair. Barely. It was clearly not built with his kind in mind. "It is only by The Wise One's grace that the children can truly be saved," the orc said. His words caused a confused look on the mayor's face, similar to that of Eldridge's earlier.

Alyssia walked over quickly to take a seat next to her hooded friend with an apologetic smile. "We are very appreciative to be here, Mayor Nahath," she said. She was thinking that if she did all of the talking, maybe she could make this work. "After what happened yesterday, Gorgron and I have been talking. He has agreed to help defend the town against the monsters in the forest," she said in a cheerful tone. She wanted to convey to Nahath that this was a *good* thing for the town even if she herself wasn't all that sure.

But after she spoke that sentence, she could see that Nahath's tired smile slowly started to fade away from his face and transition to one of concern. There was clearly a different reason as to why he had called them here today. "I... don't think that's a good idea," he said to her before he turned to speak to Gorgron. "Gorgron, this is very hard for me to say..." Nahath sighed before speaking the next sentence. "You have our thanks. Really, you do. But we cannot accept any more help from you."

Alyssia was dumbfounded. She had been rehearsing this whole interaction in her head over and over, and in none of the scenarios did this happen. She leaned forward, taking on a more serious tone. "I don't understand. You said it yourself: Gorgron saved those kids. Because of his magic, he stopped that demon singlehandedly..."

Nahath took a pause before speaking again. "I'm going to be honest, Alyssia. I'm not sure you can label what he did to that monster as... 'magic'."

Alyssia took on a more annoyed look. "I'm sorry? If not magic, then what was it then?" she questioned.

"I don't know—sorcery? Witchcraft? Necromancy? The children said the beast's *skin* melted from its bones."

Alyssia had a gut-wrenching feeling about this whole conversation. "But, Nahath, it's *all magic*. Who cares what happened to that monster when it was literally *killing children*!"

"But that's not the *point*, Alyssia," Nahath said, raising his voice a bit louder than he had intended to. "What *Pin* does is magic. He makes useful potions and elixirs for travelers and people with day-to-day needs." Nahath continued, "And even *that* makes townspeople uncomfortable. Meanwhile, that creature Gorgron touched is a skeletal husk that's currently lying in a pool of its own organs. Are you really going to tell me they're one and the same?"

Alyssia wanted so desperately to have a rebuttal, but any words that she had tried to form, quickly died in her throat. Most people in this town didn't understand the subtle complexities of magic. Even what most would deem as 'evil' magic could still be used for good in some way. But she doubted she was going to be able to convince him in one short conversation. She sat back in her chair, feeling defeated. But after some thought, she spoke again, "I'm just asking you to think about it. Imagine how many guardsmen it would have taken to stop that monster yesterday." She looked over at Gorgron, who sat there with a stoic expression through all of this. "Gorgron did it by himself. He's an asset to the town, and with his ability, we might stand a chance against them." She could tell from the look on the mayor's face that he wanted to believe this, but he shook his head.

"I can't even get my men to trust Gorgron," he admitted as he stood up out of his seat and went over to the window to look out at Green Haven. He watched as the citizens tried to resume their normal lives. But week by week, there were fewer and fewer people on the streets. "My men are warriors, not mages. They don't understand magic," he said. He turns to face them again. "They've heard many tales of villages and other small towns being destroyed by mindless slaughter or terrible plagues due to the use of dark magic." His expression shifts to one much more serious. It was odd to Alyssia to see him with such a look. Before the monsters, he was normally so cheerful and light-hearted. "My men don't *want* him here. And there's little I can do to change that."

Alyssia could understand why his men were cautious, but she couldn't help the feeling of thinking Gorgron was being punished for his good deed. She was starting to understand why he never interacted with anyone. "I get that we're all scared and confused right now. But if you're going to go storm into the forest and try to somehow make it all the way to the capital, you're going to need a magic user. Someone with strong enough magic to actually harm those things," Alyssia argued.

There was a longer pause than she liked from the mayor before he spoke again. "I agree. That's why we have a magic user already."

The red-skinned elf's ears twitched as she raised a curious eyebrow. "Huh? What, did you hire, *Thorne*? There's no one in town that's good enough with magic to take a battalion through a forest full of monsters." She had figured he was just bluffing her, but when he didn't respond, she knew he was serious. It was then that she started to put two and two together, and she didn't like the conclusion she came to. "Whoa, No. No, Mayor Nahath, please. Don't tell me you're bringing Pin into this."

"Pin is a prodigy," he responded. "He's caught on quickly and has already learned several effective combat spells just in the last few weeks alone. He will be our mage for the mission."

Alyssia's patience and capacity to still be cordial were dwindling quickly. She frowned as it was her turn to raise her voice. "Are you joking!? Pin is a potion maker. He's not a mage. He doesn't know the first thing about using magic for combat." She grit her teeth. "And he's just a kid! You're going to get him killed doing this!"

"*Pin* is a grown man who can make his own decisions." Nahath retorted. "We are doing the best we can with what we have. I don't have a lot of options or time."

There was a silence that fell across the entire room. The atmosphere was so thick that it felt like it could be cut with a knife. Nahath turned to Gorgron. "Gorgron, while I owe you a debt, I'm in a predicament. My guardsmen don't trust you to come with us, and my town has turned their backs against you."

Gorgron, now finally participating in the conversation, decided to speak with a nod of his head. "Hmph. Very well. Then I will leave by sun." The way the orc spoke made it seem as if he had just decided to take a stroll around town. It was so casual. So matter of fact. Alyssia was surprised at both of them but focused her attention on the mayor. "Wait. Mayor Nahath, you've gotta realize just how crazy all this is. You're going to kick him out *AFTER* he saved the kids?"

"He doesn't have to leave. But I need him to make a promise to me and the people," Nahath said as his eyes stayed locked on the orc. "Gorgron, I want you to promise me that there will be no consequences to my town or my people by us relying on your magic for aid. If you can just promise me that, then you do not have to leave. Maybe if we have you speak to them on a public forum, you may even be able to ease their fears of you…"

There was a stillness in the room after that. Even the shifting of Eldridge's armor as he adjusted his position rang loud and echoed off the walls. Gorgron finally opened his mouth to speak. "Whatever happens to this town will only be decided by the mercy of The Wise One's will. I will promise them nor you, nothing."

After he said that, Alyssia's shoulders dropped, and she lost every bit of her resolve on the matter. Looking disappointed, Nahath spoke again. "While I'm saddened, I must admit, you're an honest man, Gorgron. You have earned my respect." The mayor moved to go back to his desk to take a seat. A mere moment after that, Gorgron decided to stand up. "How far is the walk to the capital?"

The mayor was caught a little off guard. It took a few seconds for him to respond. "Uh. It's about a three days journey on foot through the forest. Or at least it was before the monsters."

The orc gave a nod of his head and turned to leave. "Then I will go there first. When I get there, I will send word. The mages in the capital should have a spell for long-distance communication."

All three of them, Alyssia, the mayor, and Eldridge, shared glances as the orc didn't give any of them a chance to respond. He walked out past Eldridge, giving him a nod before he left.

Alyssia shared a few uneasy glances at Nahath before she decided to leave as well. She thanked the mayor for his time and bid farewell to Eldridge. The whole conversation had done far more to annoy her than offer any kind of comfort. When she finally caught up with Gorgron, she placed a hand on his shoulder to hopefully help slow his pace. "Hey, hold up for a minute, would you? Geez, you move fast when you want to. Why'd you walk out like that?"

He did slow down to a halt, but he had this focused look in his eye that wasn't there before, she noticed. "We had no more to discuss."

He had to be the most confusing person she had ever met. How could someone be a savior but also totally deranged at the same time. "Look, I get that you can take one or maybe two of those things down by yourself. But a three-day walk? Through a forest that's full of them?" She shook her head. "Let's grab a map instead. There's probably a town or small village that's a little closer. We could—"

"And what would that do?" Gorgron said, blatantly interrupting.

"What would it do? It would prove that you could survive in the forest without dying. And maybe you could bring back some supplies or more soldiers before the mayor and the guardsmen depart in four days." She felt like she was speaking to herself here. Gorgron didn't even make eye contact with her.

"Any other small town that's closer could be in the same position we are," Gorgron said. "And they won't have elite fighting soldiers or powerful magic users to lend us. This is why Nahath wants to get to the capital. It is the only place with the right resources readily available."

Alyssia wanted to pull at her hair. "Ugh! Yes, I get it!" She groans in frustration. "But you're bleeding through your bandages still. You're going to die *well* before you get to the capital! Don't you get that?" she explains. "Or here's an idea; why not just take the mayor's offer? Just explain to the people you're not crazy so that *MAYBE* they might trust you."

After she said those words, it was only then that the orc turned to address her.

"That creature I killed yesterday was not some random, feral beast, Alyssia," he said. "It was a demon." Alyssia felt a chill run down her spine when the orc spoke those words. She had never encountered a demon before, but there were many tales and legends surrounding the vicious creatures. They were demented beings that loved the taste of mortal flesh and thrived on chaos. But them being here didn't make sense. From what she understood, they were normally only summoned through blood sacrifices and ancient rituals.

While she was still wrapped up in her thoughts, Gorgron spoke again, "If we do not get to the capital, we are *all* going to die. And I am better off trying to get there alone."

The very harsh realization of Gorgron's words struck hard at Alyssia. She closed her eyes and took in an unsteady breath. She couldn't imagine the thought of seeing those horrific creatures continuing to slaughter these people one by one.

"There is something I need to show you. Follow me." Gorgron, not waiting for her to follow, simply walked in the other direction. It took her several moments, but eventually, she followed. The two of them walked together across Green Haven until they came across a small house. It was unoccupied, but Alyssia recalled that a family had lived there at one point. They had decided to move a few months ago before the monsters began to emerge. She didn't realize at the time just how lucky they were to get out when they did. But sometimes, she wondered if they ever made it to the next town safely. Gorgron opened the door to the empty home and took a step inside first, with Alyssia following behind him afterward.

Almost as soon as she moves into the house, Alyssia covers her mouth to muffle her surprise. There, on one of the empty walls in the living room, was what she could only describe as something similar to a pentagram. A pentagram with many, many stars to the point that it looked like a chaotic mess. The odd, drawn-on symbol had this dark red color to it that looked almost like blood that had been drying on a surface for too long.

The orc made his way over to the symbol and placed his hand on it. "This is the start of a spell," he said as he looked back to Alyssia. "And

The Wise One has shown me that when the time comes, it will be of great benefit to you."

This whole thing felt crazy to Alyssia. She could feel her chest begin to tighten all of a sudden. She wanted to speak, but she struggled to get any words out. Her heart started to beat faster, and she took in big gasps of air while she placed a hand on her chest for some sense of stability. Gorgron didn't seem to take much notice of her predicament, and he just continued to speak unabated.

"The spell is activated with blood," Gorgron explained. He demonstrated by taking a knife out of his pocket and cutting open his palm horizontally. When he did this, he didn't even flinch. It was as if he could not feel the pain or had experienced it so many times before that it barely registered as pain anymore.

His blood fell on the empty living room's wooden floor from his palm. Small droplets of red dripped by his feet. "Cut your hand horizontally. Not vertically," Gorgron said as he lifted his palm and showed her the way he cut it. "And then place your hand on the symbol like so." The orc placed his hand on the pentagram. Defying all sense of logic, the dark red symbol started to illuminate, brightening the whole room in red, fluorescent light.

Alyssia felt like she couldn't breathe. Her breaths got more audible with each intake of air. "I— I can't do this," she said, taking several steps back, almost tripping over her own feet. She was trying to get to the door. Gorgron looked confused. He was completely unaware of how bizarre and out of the ordinary the entire scene looked. "Can't do it? But it's a very simple spell. Trivial really—"

"The hell is wrong with you? I'm not *doing any of this!*" She screamed out. She clutched at her chest. Was she having a panic attack? "I— I need some air." She stumbled her way toward the door.

"Hm. Perhaps you should lay down," she heard the orc say. But she didn't care. She had to get away from the entire situation. She left the house and walked several houses away before stopping to lean against an empty, nearby hay wagon. She felt like she was going to pass out. But thankfully, after a few minutes, her breathing became less labored.

Eventually, she would find herself going back to Mace and Tulips. It was packed despite the fact that it was late in the afternoon. It seems like the mayor's speech had a profound effect on the population for better or for worse. Her attention was caught by Thorne, who waved from behind the bar. "How'd it go wit' the mayor?!" The dwarf asked as he poured liquor into a glass for the patron in front of him.

"Oh, it was fantastic!" She yelled from across the room as she walked toward the steps. She didn't care to make eye contact with Thorne, and he could tell she wasn't in a good mood.

"Went dat bad, eh?" Throne said. He watched her walk past the bar and go upstairs. Thankfully for her, it was so busy he decided he wouldn't pester her about it yet. The elf would make it to her room, closing the door behind her and immediately flopping onto the bed. She would help Throne down at the bar later. For the moment, she needed to just lie down and clear her head.

Alyssia didn't talk to Gorgron again before he left. She didn't get up the next morning to see him off. No one did. He simply disappeared into the forest at the crack of dawn. No horse, no supplies. Just the book he always kept with him. Most people were excited to see him go, but some had hoped he would return as it gave hope to the idea that the guardsmen would make it back too.

Days went by, but there was no word from him. No one knew if he was dead or not, so the mayor's plans still remained the same. Alyssia couldn't help the twisting knots she felt in her stomach every moment leading up to the day that they were going to journey toward the capital.

Chapter Three

Pin woke in his bed, sat up, and did a long morning stretch. He then grabbed his glasses off the nightstand before heading over to the window to open the curtain and get a look outside. It was a nice, sunny day out. The birds were singing, and the grass was a nice, healthy shade of green. He had the thought that today was going to be a good day. That is, until the realization of what day it was hit him.

Today was the day, wasn't it? Today was the day he was going with the guardsmen to attack the beasts in the forests. He didn't want to do this, but he had a responsibility. As one of the only citizens of the town that truly understood magic, he had to do what he could to protect Green Haven. Magic was a practice that took years to learn. It wouldn't be as simple as just letting somebody read a few books and then sending them on their way. It could take some people a really long time just to learn the basics. Otherwise, they could be a danger to themselves or others. He was the only one that could do this.

He spent some time in his room, rereading his books and double-checking the spells he had taught himself. They weren't much. Just two or three was all he had time to get a good grasp on. Battle magic was quite different from what he was used to. Conjuring the amount of flame required to start a small fire to help cook dinner was different from the amount needed to immediately and effectively harm a person or monster in combat. But this journey wasn't meant to be an all-out war. Just a test run to see how they would fare against the monsters. They would stick close to the town, not going any more than a few miles out. If they fared far better than expected, they would travel deeper into the forest. If worse, they would head back.

They hoped if they cleared enough of these demons, the creatures' numbers would dwindle, and the path out would be safer. Pin could only hope the battle spells he had learned so far would be enough.

Normally Pin wore comfortable, long robes that came to his ankles. But today, he would need something much more protective than just that.

They had offered him steel armor just like the guardsmen were going to wear, but it was too heavy and clunky. Sure, it provided protection, but he wasn't used to moving in it, and he thought it would only slow him down. Instead, he had some padded gambeson armor made for him. The color was a mixture of black and dark green. It was designed to help him blend into the forest better, they said. He was supposed to be more out of sight during combat. Just providing spells and defensive magic when necessary.

Pin stalled his departure for as long as he could, reading the spells over and over to make sure he was familiar with them.

They were set to meet at dawn, and it was already a bit past that. He couldn't let his nerves keep him here any longer. So, he nervously put on his armor, even as his hands shook uncontrollably. The gambeson almost immediately felt hot on him, but if it could save his life, he would take the trade-off of sweating a little.

Pin lived in an upstairs room above his shop. It just made life easier for him if he could get up and immediately be able to go manage his store. He made his way downstairs, where he had a small, brown carry bag that he could strap to his hip lying on the counter. Before he picked it up, he took a second or two to look around the shop. It felt odd seeing most of the shelves empty and devoid of potions. He had given most of them to the guardsmen to help increase their abilities and heal them

CHAPTER THREE

when they suffered damage. He double-checked his bag to make sure he had everything he needed. Inside there were two vials of red liquid and another that was a rounded glass jar with a corked lid full of green liquid.

He breathed out a heavy breath, trying to shake his nerves. He was terrified. And as someone who understood magic, he knew there was a limit to how much damage magic could reasonably mend or repair to the human body. He felt sweaty, and his hands were clammy, but even so, he proceeded to leave the shop.

Pin was meeting the guardsmen and Mayor Nahath at the edge of town near the forest. By the time Pin had arrived, there was naturally a large gathering of people. Family and spouses were saying goodbye to their loved ones, and Pin couldn't help but feel a twinge of jealousy. He didn't have any family in this town, nor many friends. He had chosen a small town to start his business so he could make a difference with the people and really hone his skills.

But, nowadays, he thought maybe he should have just been an apprentice at a big city like his mother wanted. It had only just occurred to him that he was getting ready to head off into battle, and if he died now, none of his family was even going to know about it.

He took another glance around and saw Eldridge was there, clad in his armor like always. The guardsman gave him a smile and regarded him briefly, but it was only for a quick glance as he was busy saying goodbye to his wife and daughter. Now that he thought about it, Eldridge's daughter was barely five years old. He wondered if the head guardsman had his own regrets about this whole thing. Was he just as nervous as he was?

This train of thought was broken by a sudden smack of a hand on his back. He almost fell forward from it. He turned his head to look behind himself and noticed it was Alyssia, giving him a big smile.

He could swear her strength was different from most women her size. Or maybe he was just weak. Either way, his back was stinging like no tomorrow.

"Pin, look at you!" She said, pulling at the gambeson he was wearing. "You're wearing armor now? Heh, you're beginning to look a lot like a real guardsman, after all!"

Pin adjusted his glasses and then rubbed the back of his head in embarrassment. "Thanks. Hopefully, I look a lot better than I feel," he said.

Alyssia gave him a pat on his shoulder. "You're going to do great out there, Pin," she assured him. But, there was a pause from her, with her smile fading a little. "Listen. Promise me that you won't be reckless out there. Just stay in the back and don't get overconfident." There was clear worry in her voice and expression, but even so, Pin couldn't help the chuckle that came from him.

Alyssia raised an eyebrow curiously. "Uh. What, did I say something funny?"

"Huh? Oh. No." He rubbed the back of his head again. "It's nothing. You just... you sound like my mother."

It was her turn to laugh. "What? You trying to say I'm old, you little runt?"

Pin shook his head with a smile on his face. "No, no, not like that. It's a good thing... I wish she were here to tell me that."

Alyssia had to hold back her tears for him. Almost immediately, she pulled him into a hug. "Just be smart. And stay safe."

Nearly right after she completed that sentence, some of the guards yelled out to Pin, "Hey, Pin! We're getting ready to head out!"

Knowing he had to leave, Alyssia let go of the hug and ruffled his hair a bit. "Hey, you got this. Just remember what I said and show those monsters whose boss."

Pin gave a confident nod in response. "Thanks, Alyssia. I guess I'll, uh. I'll see you soon..."

They both finished saying their goodbyes, and he waved to her as he ran toward the group of soldiers who were standing there waiting on him. The mayor was there as well. It was a rare sight to actually see him

CHAPTER THREE

in full knight armor like Eldridge. Pin thought it was incredible that he was actually going on this mission with them. It showed a real sense of leadership.

If this wasn't a success, he didn't even want to think about the consequences. The mayor was on a brown horse holding a lance. There were four other horse riders with their own lances as well.

"Pin," Nahath said, regarding him with a nod. "I am glad you're here. We're all ready."

It was just then that Eldridge would walk up, putting on his helmet and lowering the face plate to it. There were two rectangular-shaped eye holes cut out so he could see. Vision was limited in the helmet, but years of training had helped him adjust to it. "With Pin here, I take it we are leaving?" Eldridge asked, putting a tight grip on his own lance.

"You are correct," Nahath confirmed before soon raising his lance up high in the air to get the attention of the guardsmen. "MEN!" Nahath yelled. There was a roar from the guardsmen in unison. Pin stayed quiet, however, and actually jumped a little at the sudden noise.

The mayor strode past the group on his brown horse, and the other horseback riders with lances followed.

"It will be my honor to ride into hell with you!" another loud war battle cry erupted from his men.

"Horse riders will be upfront. Eldridge, infantry, and supplies will take the middle. Pin and I will bring up the rear." As he spoke, the group started to reposition. He left a pause for them to comprehend everything he was saying before he continued. "We will be heading into the forest for about three miles. We will clear what we can and will only continue if we feel comfortable doing so. Are there any questions?"

He gave some more time for them to speak.

Only one of the guardsmen did. He was carrying a large shoulder bag full of the potions that Pin had created. "Just one. Why do *I* have to be the one carrying this?" He said, clearly annoyed by the weight of it.

The other guards couldn't help but laugh in amusement. "Why can't the *wizard-in-training* carry it? He's the magic guy," he said, with a little venom in his voice.

But Nahath responded in a calm and peaceful manner, like always. "Because, Blaise. Pin needs free range of movement."

"Oooh. 'Free range of movement'. Is that right?" The sarcastic guardsman said, swiftly going over to Pin and putting him in an uncomfortable headlock with his free arm. "Boy needs so much 'free range' just to toss about a couple of spells?" Blaise laughed. "I say we just down about five or six of these bad boys now. I want to head in breathing lightning and fartin' fire."

Some guards weren't the biggest fan of his antics, but all of them had issues stifling their laughter.

Feeling embarrassed, Pin broke free of his hold and quickly adjusted his glasses. "That would be a bad idea," he started. "The potions *are* magic based, but they do have their drawbacks." Pin continued, "Using too many in a small amount of time could have negative effects on the body. We should only use them when necessary."

While Pin was one of the youngest in the group, he did have the best understanding when it came to magic. The guardsmen gave his words proper respect.

All except for Blaise, who rolled his eyes. "Ahh, whatever."

"Alright, men. Enough!" Nahath yelled, deciding to get everyone's attention before they got too distracted with other antics. "You know your positions! Move out!" The guardsmen all hoorayed again in response. Pin, however, swallowed nervously as he saw the mayor on top of his horse with his lance pointed toward the forest. This triggers the guardsmen to move ahead in unison, heading toward the unknown and into the wilderness. Pin stayed in the back as planned, along with the mayor on his horse. It was the beginning of the afternoon, but the forest cast many shadows due to its thick leaves and branches. The road was

CHAPTER THREE

paved, making it easier for the group to traverse.

They had expected to face opposition immediately, but there were none. Not even a single monster or creature in sight. They managed to get a good mile into the forest without any resistance whatsoever. After that, they did another mile. And then another. It was like there were never any monsters there to begin with. After quite some time had gone by, Nahath decided everyone should take a break for a while. They already had gone further than they had anticipated, and they had horses pulling supplies from wooden wagons as well as men in full battle armor. It was not wise to go without rest.

Many men were relieved, thinking that maybe the monsters had gone away and found another town to prey on. Eldridge, however, was always on constant guard, thinking an ambush could happen at any moment.

During this downtime, many were quiet for one reason or another, and everyone kept themselves occupied to still the constant uneasiness they felt from being here. Some were quadruple-checking supplies. Others were sharpening their blades repeatedly. Several could be seen just staring off into the distance at nothing. Their eyes appeared to be glued to a particular tree or shadow along the forest floor.

A quiet stillness had befallen the group for a long time. That was until one of the men leaned over to whisper to one of his fellow guardsmen. "Hey. You smell that?" To get a better idea of what he was talking about, the other man raised the face plate of his helmet and smelled the air. "Actually... Yeah. It kinda smells like pie?"

A couple of men started to take notice of the conversation, and more and more began to chime in.

"I smell something too."

"What is that?"

"I think it's cinnamon...."

Soon, men began to take off their helmets completely and sniffed the air around them. They became obsessed with whatever this odd, new fragrance was. Compulsion took over a number of them, and they started wandering off in different directions, attempting to find the source of the smell. Soon, over a dozen men had strayed far from the camp. So far, in fact, they had disappeared into the darkness of the many trees that surrounded them.

Pin had been sitting by himself, with his face buried inside one of his books. He hadn't been paying attention at all to what was going on. He was just thankful he had more time to read up on his spells. It was only when one of the guardsmen touched his shoulder that his attention was drawn away from his studies. "Huh?" he said, confused at the sudden intrusion of his space.

"You smell that?" the man asked him curiously.

"Smell what?" Pin asked, shifting in place uncomfortably. The man was getting unnecessarily close to him. "How could you not smell it? It smells like... roses and incense." the guardsman's voice spoke with intent, but his eyes looked glossed over as if he was half awake. It was just then that Blaise came over and interrupted them. He had a handkerchief covering his nose. "Hey! Actually, I think they just found the source of it over there," he said as he pointed in the direction of a group of guardsmen that had gathered together. "Did they?" The troop replied, his voice sounding thrilled at the notion. His expression didn't change, though. It was still dull and emotionless. Slowly, he walked away to join the other guards.

Once he had left, Blaise threw a cloth to Pin.

"Quick, boy. Put this over your mouth and nose," Blaise whispered. By this point, over half the men were obsessed with whatever they were smelling. A couple even got on their knees, attempting to sniff the ground like a common dog.

"I—I don't understand," Pin said as he looked around at the other men before covering his nose with the cloth. "What's going on?" When Pin asked that, he could see Blaise frown from underneath the cloth he had covering his face. He had removed his helmet completely, revealing his long, bristly black hair.

"*Pay Attention!*" Blaise yelled with an annoyed tone. "You got your face buried so deep in that book you don't even see what's going on around you. Get up!" He grabbed Pin's collar and yanked him up to his feet. "I don't know if it's some kind of hysteria or spell or whatever. Either way, most of 'em have lost their minds." He gestured in the direction of the town's mayor, who was just sitting there on top of his horse. His eyes looked glossed over, and his head raised to the sky at nothing. A few of the men had come over to him, trying to ask questions or get him involved, but he did nothing.

"We're sittin' ducks out here. T'way I see it, we got two options: die with them or we head toward the capital. Just you and me." He points down the paved trail. "If we take a horse and some rations, we just might make it by ourselves," he said.

"You mean we're— we're just going to *abandon them*?" Pin said as his mind started to race. How did things go from being okay to this in what seemed to be such a short span of time? "When I became a guardsman, I took a vow. I—I can't just abandon the mission." Pin looked around frantically, trying to look for someone he could latch onto for advice or to at least affirm what he was saying.

"Screw the vow!" Blaise spat to his side. "Think about it; if it's one of those monsters doing it, we're already dead. And if it's hysteria, it's only a matter of time before we get caught out here like sitting ducks. *We failed!*" As Blaise said these words, the harsh reality of the situation started to seep into Pin's mind. The young magic user began to take in quick, short breaths as panic sat in.

"Okay, listen. I'm going to explain this slowly to you." He sighed and took in a deep breath. It was hard to remain calm as he knew they were on a severe time limit. "I get what the mayor told us. But it's only a three-day journey if you're traveling in a large group like us or on foot," he said.

"If we take a horse, we might get there a lot quicker." Blaise gestures to one of the guardsmen on horseback. He had a cloth over his nose in one hand and the reigns of the horse in the other. He was trying his best to keep the dull-eyed men from wandering too far away. It was as if he was hoarding sheep. "See that guy over there? On my mark, we're going to knock him down, take his horse and get the hell out of here. Ready?"

Pin's eyes hastily shifted from Blaise to the man on horseback. He barely had the mental capacity to think at the moment. Blaise started counting. "Alright. One... two—"

"Blaise!" Eldridge stepped in, cutting the count off early.

The sound of Eldridge's voice was like a breath of fresh air for Pin. It felt like oxygen finally started to enter his lungs properly. Just like Blaise and Pin, he had a cloth up to his face. "What are you doing!?"

Blaise had the biggest smirk spread across his features as he placed a hand on Pin's shoulder. "I'll tell you what. My boy Pin and I are getting out of this hellhole," Blaise said. Although Pin looked too uncomfortable to properly protest and Eldridge could see that.

"No, you are not," Eldridge said in a firm tone. "I and the guardsmen not affected by the smell are regrouping and attempting to help the others." Eldridge turned his attention to Pin. "Pin, can you learn a spell on the spot?"

It took Pin a second to answer. He had just been on a whirlwind of different emotions. He swallowed hard before nodding his head. "Y-yeah. I think so."

"Good. I need you to look through your book and find a sleep spell. Maybe if we put the men to sleep, we can take them back to town and—"

Blaise interrupts. "You two really gonna sit here and try to save these schmucks?" he asked. "Listen. Screw you and screw the kid, Eldridge. I'm getting outta here."

Before Eldridge could respond to him, one of the guardsmen yelled out at the top of his lungs.

CHAPTER THREE

"Everyone! I found it! I found the smell!" At that moment, everyone immediately looked over. The man who had yelled was standing in front of a tree, looking up at it as if in a trance. The tree he was looking at was twisted and distorted. Its bark looked like it had been spun around itself many times. In front of where the man stood, the wood seemed to deform and appeared to crack and separate. The tree looked as if it was forming a mouth similar to that of a person's. A haunting maw that opened and released a rush of pleasant smells that lured more of the men to stand in front of it.

As the men stood in awe, small creatures emerged from within the shadows of the forest. They were grotesque two-legged monsters, no more than two feet tall. They had no eyes but many rows of fanged teeth. Their large mouths appeared to make up the majority of their small bodies. These hideous monstrosities began to jump and climb up any man who stood in front of the tree and currently wasn't wearing a helmet or had their face plates up.

The monsters began to bite and tear at the exposed flesh on their faces. Their large jaws easily ripped skin and meat from the bone. The men did nothing to stop the assault. No screams or wailing terror. They just stood there, with their dull expressions unwavering as the monsters ate away at them.

The sight caused even the men who weren't affected to have several moments of pause. Blaise was the first one to react.

"Screw all of ya!" he yelled. While everyone was distracted, he ran over to the guardsman on the horse that he pointed to earlier. He proceeded to knock him off and take it from him. Seconds later, he could be seen riding down the paved forest path, the horse striding at full gallop. Eldridge thought about stopping him, but there were far more pressing matters. "Pin!" he called over to jolt the young man out of his shock. "Burn the tree! Quickly!"

His words snapped Pin out of the daze he was in from watching the horrific scene. "O-oh. Yeah. Right!" Pin managed to stutter out before he cupped his hands together, making a sort of sphere out of them. Sparks of red magic started to ignite within his palms until a ball of fire was floating between his hands. Just casting this one spell took a lot of focus to achieve. Beads of sweat were already forming on his forehead.

He threw the flame he had just created at the tree, quickly igniting it in a blaze. The tree itself let out a scream through its mouth that could only be described as an ear-piercing wail. It screams and writhes in place, embers of flame dropping from all around it, including onto the men and small creatures below. Because the fire was magical in nature, as soon as it touched anything else, it lit that aflame as well. The small, hideous creatures stood no chance against the flames due to their small size. Their bodies burned up quickly, and fell to the ground. However, the men who were nearby— even the ones who had come over to help fend off the little creatures—were also lit on fire.

The guardsmen who were in a trance, didn't even let out a scream or try to run. They merely stood in place with the flames engulfing them. The other guardsmen tried rolling on the ground to get the fire off themselves.

Eldridge could do little but watch as his men burst into flames. He diverted his gaze from the nightmarish scene and turned his attention back to Pin. "Pin! Stop this! Stop the fire!" Even someone like Eldridge was beginning to lose his composure.

Pin gripped his own head with both of his hands. Tears were beginning to form in his eyes. "I— I can't! Once I release the spell, I don't know how to stop it!" He'd only had a few weeks to learn what he knew. He didn't know how to neutralize his magic whatsoever. And thus, the two of them could do nothing but watch as the tree, along with the many guardsmen near it, were immersed in a blaze. The guardsmen who were not near the tree were beginning to lose focus on the mission. It was like it was every man for themselves. They took supplies, stole horses, and

CHAPTER THREE

began to scatter in different directions.

Attempting to cling onto whatever hope the mission still had, Eldridge ran over to the mayor to hopefully shake him out of his daze. By this point, the mayor had finally gotten off his horse. "Sir! These men need guidance!" He pleaded. "We need you to say something! Anything! Help me to rally them!" As Eldridge continued to talk, he felt as if he was speaking to a husk. The look on the mayor's face was that of a broken man. He wasn't fit to lead or rally anyone. It looked like he had been crying, but there were no tears visibly falling down his cheeks.

Eldridge had an overwhelming urge to slap or hit the man. Partly because he hoped it would awaken him from this state but mostly because he thought the mayor had failed him and his men. Instead though, he turned away from him, simply leaving the broken mayor there so he could go back to Pin. But he wasn't in the best state either. Pin's eyes were dancing in different directions, and he was taking short, rapid breaths as if he was hyperventilating. Despite the situation, Eldridge spoke calmly again. "Pin, listen. Focus on me. Try to stable your breathing."

Hearing those words, Pin kept his eyes focused on Eldridge as he tried to take in slow, deep breaths as best as he could.

Eldridge nodded at the development. "Okay. Good. Good Pin." He placed a hand on Pin's shoulder. "Mayor Nahath is not fit to take control of the situation any longer," he said.

While Eldridge talked to him, Pin's eyes briefly darted over to look at the mayor. Even though he looked as if he was coming over to join them again, he had a defeated look in his eyes that suggested he wasn't going to be of much use.

Eldridge continued, "It's up to us now. Let's gather the troops we can and head back."

However, shortly after he finished that sentence, a dagger pierced into the side of Eldridge's exposed neck. The sharp blade buried deep, all the way to the hilt. Any further words from Eldridge died in his throat immediately. His eyes went wide, and he spat out blood. Nahath was behind him, his hand grasping the dagger that had just stabbed the head guardsman in the neck firmly.

Pin gasped in shock as the mayor roughly jerked the dagger from Eldridge's throat, causing blood to spurt from the wound. Eldridge fell to his knees, coughing up more blood and holding onto the side of his neck. Nahath stood looking over him as the dagger he held dripped blood onto the ground. He watched as the man struggled to breathe.

"Eldridge," Nahath started. "Apologies mean nothing now, but I just want you to know that there was not a single day that I took for granted everything you did to help protect Green Haven."

It was almost in tandem with Nahath speaking that more creatures started to emerge from the forest. Among them were creatures with wings that were covered in fur. They had the size and faint resemblance of a man, but the way they moved and scurried about on the forest ground suggested anything but. They had no mouths but, in their place were long, tube-like appendages that looked almost like bee stingers.

"You've been so loyal to me over the years," Nahath said, beckoning the odd-winged beasts to come closer. They were almost like obedient children, scurrying about as they made their way over to Nahath. "The least I can do for you is make sure it's over quickly." Nahath took his dagger and was about to stab Eldridge again when suddenly half his face erupted into flames. The heat caused him to scream in agony and stumble back.

"G-get away from him!" Pin yelled. He stood in front of Eldridge to get in between them. His hands were cupped in a sphere shape like before as he worked to create another fireball to throw at him.

Nahath patted at the fire frantically to put it out. It took him far longer to subside the flames than it would have normally due to their magical nature. More than half of his face was severely burned and charred black from the heat by the time the fire had stopped burning. Any other person

CHAPTER THREE

would have been unable to speak or even stand up straight after such catastrophic burns, but Nahath just gave a hearty laugh as he shifted his gaze to Pin now. "Wow. And to think you *just* learned that spell a few weeks ago. You're a real prodigy, Pin."

The creatures from before made their way to Nahath's side, standing next to him like obedient dogs awaiting orders.

Pin's brain had issues putting together and fathoming what he was seeing. Nothing over the past minute had made any sense to him. His hands wouldn't stop shaking. "A-are you... *controlling these things*!?" Even as Pin said those words, there was a clear sound of disbelief in his voice. How was this even possible.

"These demons have pledged their loyalty to me, Pin," Nahath said as he made a simple gesture to the monsters beside him. It didn't take much to command them. It was as if their thoughts were aligned with his. With a simple wave of his hand, they spread their wings and flew off in different directions. "But loyalty comes at a price."

The beasts flew after the few men who were still nearby, as well as all the guardsmen who were trying to escape. The men could do little to fend off the hideous beasts as they ripped through their heavy armor like paper. The demons used their stinger-like appendages akin to that of mosquitos as they punctured the skin of the fleeing guardsmen and started to extract blood from them. There were screams of agony coming from near and far as the once fit and healthy men began to become unnaturally frail and decrepit. It was as if every ounce of moisture was painstakingly being extracted from their body.

After observing such a horrific scene from all around him, Pin was terrified. He remained in place, not as some defiant and brave hero, but as a trembling coward. He was unable to even run as his knees looked like they could give out from under him at any second. Looking back on it now, Pin realized they never stood a chance against these creatures from the beginning. Near the entire militia of guardsmen had been killed in just a few minutes by these creatures. This was a suicide mission.

Even as Pin's mind was reeling from what was going on around him, Nahath started to speak. "You see this, Pin? This is all we are to them. Just food. Playthings," he said, as the horrible noises of blood and gore going on around them only served to amplify his words like a symphony of horror. "And with the promise of enough *flesh a*nd human souls, they'll do just about anything I want them to."

It was then that other hideous and mysterious creatures started to emerge from the forest around them, but there was one that was particularly huge. It looked to be about as tall as most of the houses back in Green Haven. It stood bipedal on two legs, but it looked like a black mass with no distinguishable face or features outside of two piercing white eyes that easily cut through the shadowy forest.

Having seen so many demons, Pin gave up trying to cast his fireball spell. The flames dissipated between his palms, and he let his hands flop helplessly to his side. "I— I don't get it," Pin said, his voice beginning to crack from the impending tears he couldn't stop from forming. The betrayal he felt at this exact moment was overwhelming. Crushing. "Why did you have me learn combat magic? Why put me through all of this just to kill me?"

"Because, Pin, sometimes different demons require different terms to summon them," Nahath answered as he made another gesture. This time it was the dark, featureless titan that would step forward. "And this one prefers the flesh of a mage," he said.

"PIN!" Eldridge's blood-gurgling call cut in on their conversation. He was still on his knees, blood trickling from his lips and pouring out of his throat. He had a hand clutching at his neck to help slow the bleeding. "Run!" He tried to get up, but just the act of breathing was difficult. There was little else he could do but yell.

His words helped Pin's shaky legs finally receive some strength. Quickly, he goes to run, but it wasn't long before he felt a presence suddenly behind him, followed by a large formless mass slamming into his body. When the featureless demon moved, it didn't make a sound or cast a shadow despite its size. It was like it barely existed.

If it hadn't been for the fact that the hit knocked the wind out of him, he would have screamed from the pain. He felt some of his bones crack when the mass landed. Pin struggled to get air as the expressionless, shapeless being gradually reached out to pick up his limp body. Its prehensile limb was so distorted and obscure, it would have been erroneous to compare it to anything resembling human. Part of the titan's blank face slowly split apart, revealing an empty void that could have been considered a mouth.

As this was happening, Nahath **walked** over to Eldridge, looking down on him, not with triumph, but with pity. He watched him struggle for breath and continue to bleed out onto the dirt. The mayor crouched down next to him. "Eldridge, there wasn't anything you could have done for him," Nahath said as his gaze moved upward to look at the titan as it gradually began to devour Pin. He could do little but attempt to struggle against its hold while he was swallowed into the dark abyss of the creature's maw, disappearing until there was nothing left of him.

When it was over, Nahath addressed Eldridge again. "In spite of everything...I just don't have it in me to let you be eaten by these monsters, Eldridge," he said, resting a hand on Eldridge's shoulder plate. "I'm going to let you have some final moments of peace to yourself. And when I bring the demons back to Green Haven, I'm going to do my best to steer them away from Sarah and Molly."

Nahath wouldn't get words from Eldridge anymore. He would only be met with a defiant glare that was accompanied by a spit of blood against the charred part of his face. Nahath didn't retort. Instead, he **stood** to his feet and casually walked over to the horse he rode into the forest on. He **hopped** onto the back of it in a swift motion. Nearly every guardsman who went into the forest by that point was either dead or dying. There was very little the town could do to stand up to these monstrosities. "Demons! Leave these dying men behind! There is plenty more food back in Green Haven!" He commanded as he took off on his horse in a full gallop back toward town.

Like children, the hideous beasts followed, leaving Eldridge and the rest of the dying men to their fate.

Chapter Four

Alyssia had just bought some fruit from the local market and was sitting at the edge of town, taking a few bites out of an apple. She had been worried sick about the battalion ever since they left and just couldn't calm her nerves down. Night was approaching as they were in the final moments of dusk. The sky was still a dull, orange color, with the sun leisurely settling beneath the trees. Alyssia's thoughts wandered. Was Pin okay? Did they decide to keep going? Her stomach was in knots while she sat there staring at the forest, half expecting them to come back.

For a second, her eyes lost focus on the forest and trailed down to the dirt below. She had been out there long enough. She had to open the bar in the morning. The red elf moves to stand when suddenly she hears the faint sounds of horse hooves hitting dirt in the distance. She immediately dropped the apple onto the grass below when she noticed Nahath on his horse riding back at full speed. Excitedly, she gave him a big smile and a welcoming wave. "Nahath! Hey! Hey, welcome back! How did it... go..." her voice trailed off when she started to pay closer attention to what she was seeing. She noticed that something wasn't quite right about the mayor's face, and once he got a few yards closer, she could tell that half of it had been completely blackened and burned.

And the horrendous figures that were moving next to him... They weren't Pin or the guardsmen. She could tell instantly that the monstrosities were not human. She froze. But for only a second this time. She didn't know what was going on, but she knew she had to warn the people. She turned heel and ran back toward the town as fast as she could. She started yelling at the top of her lungs for whoever would listen. "EVERYONE! RUN! DEMONS ARE HERE!" she screamed.

The faces of the people immediately turned to panic. They dropped whatever they were doing and began to run or escape into their fortified houses.

Someone else shouted, "Alert the guards! Alert the ones who are still here!" There were at least a dozen or so guardsmen left behind to protect the people.

Alyssia ran through the town, yelling at the top of her lungs to warn the townspeople. Not a single one ignored her warning as they locked themselves inside and started to board up their doors. When she got about halfway through Green Haven, she heard the sounds of people screaming in the distance. And when she looked over head, there were dozens of winged demonic creatures flying in the skies above her. The demons were already in town. One even tried to swoop down and grab at her with its talons, but she jumped out of the way just before it dug its sharp claws into her.

Frustrated, the creature shifted focus and grabbed a citizen nearby. The man yelled in pain when the dark claws dug into his shoulders, and he was lifted away soon after. Not knowing where to go, Alyssia made her way to the plaza. The sounds of people screaming and being attacked echoed all around her as her mind was racing with how she could possibly help them all.

Hopelessness swept over her and caused her not to even notice the terrible creature that loomed closer. It was giant and all black with glowing white eyes. When it walked, there was no noise. It had no presence. Before she realized it, the monster had grabbed her and flung her across the town square. Her body landed rough against the cold, stone road. A groan of pain escaped her. She felt dizzy, and her vision blurred. As she struggled to get to her feet, she could do nothing but watch as the large beast wreaked havoc on anyone who was running by the square. They were given the same harsh treatment as if they were just toys to the demon.

Some people were stomped on by the monster, their bodies crushed beneath the weight of its mass. Others were thrown like Alyssia had been, though their bodies hadn't been as resilient. Some were thrown high up and landed on their heads, crushing their skulls on impact. The power and speed with which it threw several others caused bones and limbs to break.

The town square was rapidly becoming a blood bath. Several guardsmen had come over, attempting to cut at the creature with their swords, but little came of it. The monster didn't even appear to register as being cut. Perhaps it couldn't feel pain at all. Their armor did not protect in the slightest against the creature, and after the second guardsman was crushed inside of his armor, the other few fled.

The creature gave chase behind the fleeing guardsmen, which prompted Alyssia to look around for something she could use as a weapon. Nearby was an axe lying on the ground from the local woodcutter's workshop. She ran over to pick up the axe and, without having much time to think, haphazardly threw it at the demon. The speed and ferocity at which she threw the axe surprised even her. Thorne had always said she was as strong as an ox, but she had never felt the need to test those limits until now.

The axe embedded itself inside the titan's mid-section, causing it to pause and stop focusing on the guards. It turned its focus on her now. The creature looked incapable of showing any emotion, but the noise it made could only be described as a long, reoccurring echo. Similar to what one might experience inside an old, abandoned cave.

The demon made its way toward her now. Terrified, Alyssia ran. She ran as fast as she could with the creature giving chase. She had no strategy or plan on how to deal with the monster. This was all she could do to help the people here; just be a distraction to keep it from killing anyone else. The harrowing part of the ordeal was having to repeatedly look behind herself as she ran. The creature made no noise when it moved, so the only way to know if it was getting closer was to physically look back to see where it was. The demon chased after her quickly, but it wasn't running in any traditional sense. Instead, it's body just seemed to rapidly vibrate and shift forward at a rapid rate.

She tried to go down narrow alleyways, but the monstrosity's form was malleable. Despite its size, it would squeeze and adjust its shape to fit into any pathway she went down without losing speed. She ran with everything she had. Her lungs and legs were on fire, but the being that chased her appeared to be unable to fatigue. Quickly, it got within arms distance and was mere moments away from reaching out and grabbing her with one of its appendages when instead, it appeared to just… stopped. It was like it was frozen in time. Alyssia only had it in her to sprint another few blocks before her body forced her to stop. She was going to pass out if she ran any longer.

She took big gasps of air as she looked back at the creature with confusion. Why did it stop? Another ten seconds or so, and she would've been as good as dead. The black mass let out another drawn-out echo, but this time the noise was deafening. So much so that she had to cover her ears from the sound.

It was just then that the mid-section of the being erupted outwards. A sudden rush of black goo exploded out from what appeared to have been its stomach. Some odd seconds later, the beast fell forward and crashed into the ground. The white glow of its eyes had faded completely.

While her mind tried to wrap itself around what had just happened, she noticed that one of the piles of goo that came out of the creature actually moved. Groaned even. She was hesitant as she made her way over to it, and it was only after closer inspection that she saw that it was—
"Pin!?" She screamed in confusion.

What was he doing *inside* of that thing? She immediately went down to her knees to get a closer look at him. Whatever explosion had taken place inside of the monster had hit him too. His face was covered in heavy burns, and a good chunk of his gambeson was seared off. He looked like he was barely responsive.

"My... bag," she heard him say weakly. It was almost inaudible. In fact, it took a second for her to even register what had been said. He was covered in black ooze, but she remembered seeing where his bag was before he left. She peeked inside of it, and thankfully there were two vials of potions full of red liquid in there.

She recognized what they were. She had recalled him saying at one point that these types of potions would be useful for repairing injuries. "I know you're big on the whole potion usage thing, but I think you'll forgive me for using two instead of one," she said as she helped hold his head up so that he could drink. With each gulp of the elixir, his wounds started to mend, and his burns began to gradually disappear. Eventually, after drinking both potions, he was able to sit up on his own. He clutched his head in his hand. He had a throbbing migraine and was still clearly disoriented.

Alyssia didn't waste time, though. Now that he was feeling better, she got to her feet and started to pull Pin up to his. "Pin, I know you feel like crap, but we have to move. There're way too many demons around."

Even with the potions, he was still a little shaky getting to his feet. "Alyssia. The mayor... he— he set us up. He's *working with the demons.*"

Alyssia put Pin's arm over her shoulder to help him walk. It was her worst nightmare come true, but she had to stay focused. They were like sitting ducks out in the open. "Pin, save your strength. Come on."

There was only one house nearby that wasn't boarded up by now, and it was the one she dreaded going into again. Hastily, she and Pin walked toward the home. They were lucky enough that most demons were already preoccupied trying to rip through the doors or burst through the windows of other houses to get to the people inside. They hadn't taken notice of the duo moving past.

When they finally arrived inside the empty house, Alyssia closed the door and locked it behind them. But she wasn't so naive as to think a lock was going to keep any of those monsters at bay. "Can you stand on your own now?" Alyssia asked.

"Y-Yeah, I think so," Pin answered.

"Good. Then help me barricade the doors and windows with something." Alyssia went over to the kitchen to quickly dig through drawers in hopes of finding knives or anything else they could use as weapons.

"Yeah. Okay. I'll—" Pin's sentence died in his throat before he could finish it. His eyes finally landed on the large pentagram symbol that was so plainly displayed in the living room.

"Alyssia..." he said as his breath became unsteady.

"What?" She said before she turned around to see Pin staring at the pentagram. With everything going on, it slipped her mind to warn him before they stepped in. "Oh. Pin, look, don't concentrate on that right now. We have to—"

"*Alyssia, what is this!?*" He asked, his voice raising louder this time. She could tell he was starting to freak out, so she answered calmly. "I don't know. It was something Gorgron showed me. Had to do with The Wise One or... something." She wished she had a better explanation for the insanity, but she... didn't. She saw Pin staring at the symbol, looking the most lost that she had ever seen him. She wondered if his mind had just stopped trying to process any of this or make sense of it. She felt like she was on the verge of feeling the same way.

"We have to leave," he said. Plainly. Calmly.

"I'm sorry... what?" Alyssia replied.

"Let's just make a run for it. Right now," Pin said, panic clearly starting to show on his face. "All the demons are probably here by now, right? If we make a run for the capital, maybe we could get a big enough head start to where they won't catch up to us," he elaborated.

Alyssia had the thought that even if they wanted to run, she doubted the likelihood that they would be able to escape far with those winged creatures circling the sky. But besides any of that— "Pin, we can't. We can't just leave everyone to be murdered by those... things."

Pin reached up and grabbed his own hair, pulling on it. "*Then we're going to die with them!*" he cried. "I only know a few spells, and we have no potions. *How are we going to stop a town full of those things?*" He broke down in tears. He covered his face and fell to his knees, sobbing. "Alyssia, I don't want to die..." he said, shamelessly bawling his eyes out.

Alyssia thought about trying to comfort him, but the worst part about it was that he was right. The two of them turning the tide on this was unlikely. And the guardsmen were just fodder for the demons. Left with no choice, Alyssia couldn't believe what she was about to say. "I— I think I might have a way to—"

It was just then that part of the roof caved in over Pin's head. Large chunks of wood and debris from the destroyed ceiling fell on top of him, trapping most of his body beneath the rubble. The cloud of dust that suddenly filled the room from the collapsed ceiling made Alyssia have to cover her nose and cough. A loud roar from overhead made her divert her eyes upward, where she saw the culprit of the destruction.

It was a giant, worm-like creature. Its gaping wide maw had so many rows and lines of teeth that she couldn't count them all. The demon peered into the hole in the ceiling it had just created, curiously. There were no eyes on the beast, but somehow, it looked to be able to sense where they were. Its attention was locked on Alyssia, and it looked like it was going to try to slither its body into the living room through the half-destroyed roof.

The creature was so big, it seemed as though it was going to collapse the entire structure of the home. Alyssia felt paralyzed. Even if she tried to run away, she would be trapped in the destruction this monster was about to make. Its body tore through more of the roof as it tried to fit its maw inside. That was when, unexpectedly, a burst of flame was shot into the creature's mouth. The beast screeched in pain from the fire and quickly withdrew from the house in retreat.

Alyssia's eyes moved over to the source of where the attack came from. It was Pin. Half his body was still buried under wood and rubble, but his hands were free enough that he was able to conjure a spell. She was taken a back a little. She hadn't realized how good he had gotten with magic. She runs over to him, coughing from all the dust and debris that had accumulated in the air. "Pin! Pin, are you okay?" Alyssia said while she frantically started to pull the debris off of him.

"Maybe? I don't know," he said. "I don't think I can move."

By the time she got more of the broken ceiling and wood off him, she noticed that one of his legs was trapped underneath a large, broken wooden beam. Alyssia inspected the partially destroyed structure but didn't see a way to pull him out from underneath it. The only way to save him was going to be to lift the wooden beam. "Okay— okay. It's alright. I got you. Just keep breathing." She took in a couple of deep breaths and exhaled a few times to get herself ready for this.

She squatted down and grabbed hold of the broken beam, gripping it tight as she started straining to lift it. Pin was shocked she would even attempt to lift such a heavy piece of construction. He doubted even a guardsmen could lift it, and they carried around fifty pounds of armor on their backs. "Alyssia, I don't know if this is going to work," he said. "Let's see if we can get some leverage another... way."

His voice began to trail off when he noticed the wooden beam began to shift and move upwards gradually. He was stunned. It was a miraculous sight to behold, watching her not only lift the beam, but move it out of the way. He was confused for a moment, but then he realized she had purchased that potion of Cyclops Strength from him not that long ago. He breathed out a sigh of relief when he was finally free to move.

CHAPTER FOUR

"Thanks, Alyssia. I thought I was a goner for sure—" he stopped speaking when the horrid look on her face caused him to pause. "What? What is it—" His eyes followed down to where her gaze had landed. It was his leg. It had been completely crushed from the rubble. Starting from a little above his knee and downward, there were fragments of broken bones as well as muscle clearly visible. His blood had made a pool of red beneath him.

It was then that he felt the pain. He screamed louder than he ever realized his lungs were capable of. There was not much Alyssia could do, medically. Even with a doctor under the best conditions, she doubted they would have a way to treat an injury this severe. "Pin, try to focus on me. What about your shop?" she asked. "Do you have any more healing potions there?"

"No!" he exclaimed. "We took all of the healing potions to the forest. I just had a few in my pouch for emergencies." He clenched his teeth hard and took in sharp breaths as he tried to put pressure on his leg to help stop the bleeding. There was so much blood already that he was afraid he was going to die of blood loss. Alyssia helped him by ripping some of his clothes that hadn't already been destroyed to use as a tourniquet.

Alyssia didn't waste any time after that. She stood up and started looking around the house. She dug through drawers, cabinets, and anything else she could search through. Pin watched her run around and began to feel increasingly confused. "Alyssia, what are you doing?"

"Finding a knife," she replied as she grabbed one of the lone kitchen knives that were in a drawer. She made her way to the front of the pentagram that Gorgron had made and took in a deep breath. "This better work like you said," she muttered to herself. She placed the sharp blade on her palm, groaning in pain and cutting deep into it horizontally just like the orc had shown her. As her blood began to drip onto the floor, she hesitantly placed her palm against the pentagram.

The blood from her wound quickly started to travel throughout the symbol by itself. It began to gradually rejuvenate and reactivate the pentagram, almost as if it was recreating it anew. Old, dried blood became fresh again, and soon, the symbol had gotten so bright that it was too blinding for her to stare at directly. She covered her eyes and stepped back a few times.

The pentagram had appeared to form some kind of bridge or portal in front of her. And from the light, she could see two silhouettes beginning to step through it as if it were a simple doorway. It was Gorgron, and with him was Eldridge, whose arm was draped over his shoulder to help him walk. The orc was carrying a large sac in his free hand while Eldridge weakly gripped his lance.

"Ahh. I see you used the spell. Just as The Wise One said you would."

Earlier

Left to bleed to death, the head of the guardsmen was holding his neck as tight as he could while sitting against a tree. The entire guardsmen were gone, Pin was dead, and he couldn't stop the wound from bleeding no matter how much pressure he applied to it. The color on his face was starting to look washed out from blood loss. Eldridge felt his heartbeat begin to slow down, and his eyes start to get heavy. Was he really about to die here? The only thing keeping him from passing out was the occasional flash in his mind of his wife and child. The thought of them being eaten by those demons was a horrid enough thought to keep him conscious, but he still didn't have the strength to get up.

He had to do something before he lost whatever small amount of energy he still had left within him. His eyes darted around the area, and he took notice of a disheveled bag that was underneath a turned-over horse wagon. This was the bag of potions they had brought with them. Part of it looked to be crushed already, so most of them probably wouldn't be usable, but there was some hope at least that he could get a potion to heal himself. But he couldn't stand. His armor was too heavy, and he wasn't able to take it off. He grit his teeth as he threw himself onto his stomach instead.

It took a considerable amount of strength to slowly crawl on his belly. The bag was only around ten yards away, but it might as well had been several thousand because he didn't get very far. He had lost enough blood that his body no longer had the strength to continue.

As he was on the verge of passing out, he noticed two large gray feet step up next to him. "The Wise One is not ready for you yet." He heard a voice say. It was almost like he had seen a ghost when he watched the orc move over toward where the sack was. The orc opened up the bag of potions and dug through it. Soon, he pulled out a potion bottle of red liquid that he brought over to the guardsmen. Gorgron rolled him over to his back and held up his head as he allowed the guardsman to drink some of the elixir. "A lot of the potions were destroyed, but some still remained," Gorgron said.

Eldridge could feel the life start to enter back into his body with each gulp of the potion. He regained some of his color again. "I thought you were dead, Gorgron," Eldridge said as he stared up at the gray orc.

"Hmph. Not dead. Just confused." Gorgron tried to tilt the rest of the potion into his mouth, but Eldridge shook his head and pushed the bottle away. He wasn't one hundred percent, but the deep cut across his neck had healed. "No. Save it," Eldridge said, not wanting to waste the precious little resources they had already. "What do you mean by confused?"

Gorgron turned his head, staring off into the distance to the path that led deeper into the forest. "There is no way to leave this town," he stated. "Two days walking distance out, there is a barrier that prevents you from going on any further. We are all trapped here."

No matter how out of character it felt, Eldridge couldn't help the laugh that escaped his lips. "Wow. So we were all doomed no matter what we did."

That statement just caused Gorgron to look even more confused. Seeing the perplexed look on his face made Eldridge explain the situation. "It's the mayor. He's working with the demons," he said as he tried to get up but was still a little wobbly on his feet. He ends up falling back onto the ground again.

"Hm. I see." On the battlefield littered with the bodies of murdered guardsmen, the orc casually walked over to a nearby tree. Eldridge had to wonder how he was able to see such a horrific scene with barely any context and not bat an eye to it. He saw the orc take a knife from his pocket and cut deep into his hand until it dripped blood on the grass below. If that wasn't odd enough, Eldridge watched him start to paint a weird symbol out of his own blood onto the tree as if he was using it as some kind of canvas with his hand's blood as the palette.

Eldridge was bewildered watching him do this. If anyone else had behaved the way Gorgron did, he would think they were a mad man. But, considering he was able to live this long by himself in a forest full of demons... it was hard to judge him as such. But that also begs the question: "How did you survive?" Eldridge asked. "You were sent out here with no food, no supplies... we all thought you were dead."

Gorgron replies to him but never turns away from what he is doing. "There is no need for food or water. The Wise One sustains."

It looked like whatever he was painting, he was doing it down to the most minute detail. But in Eldridge's eyes, it looked like a chaotic mess.

The worst part is they were low on time. They were going to need to act fast to stop Nahath, and Eldridge needed to help him realize that. "Gorgron, listen to me," he said, slowly gathering enough energy to stand properly. "Nahath has a legion of demons with him and they're heading towards the town. He plans to kill everyone." He looked around for horses, but they had either been torn to shreds or devoured by this point. They would have to trek back on foot. "We have to hurry."

"Even if we ran all the way there, we would not make it back in time," Gorgron stated while he continued to draw nonchalantly. Eldridge steps forward. "Then what do you suggest? We stay here and wait for death ourselves?"

Gorgron doesn't respond right away. He kept drawing until the odd pentagram-looking figure was complete. At least in his eyes. "No..."

The symbol he made from his own blood started to turn and twist all on its own. Soon, there was a large, bright portal that formed in the middle of the tree that continuously spread. Eldridge looked amazed at the sight. He had to cover his eyes, but Gorgron didn't appear to be bothered by the blinding light. He turned back to him.

"We follow the guidance of The Wise One..."

Present

Alyssia could barely speak she was so surprised. "But... how did you—when did you—"

"I myself did nothing. It was all The Wise One. We are merely guided to our destiny by his hand." It was at this time that Eldridge was able to finally stand on his own. His legs felt less wobbly, and he was starting to recover. Alyssia didn't care if whatever Gorgron talked about was real or fake at this point. She was just so happy to see two familiar faces. Her eyes lit up when they darted over to the sack he was holding. "Is that—are those the potions!?"

"These? Ah, yes, there were still some left out in the forest," Gorgron said.

"Please. I need all of the healing potions in there. Pin's in really bad shape." Gorgron didn't contest as Alyssia dug through all of the broken glass from the crushed potions inside to get to a proper recovery potion. With that and the other that was left over from what Eldridge didn't drink, she made her way over to Pin. Seeing Pin lying on the other side of the room made Eldridge join along with her as well. Pin looked barely conscious, but he smiled when he saw Eldridge was there.

"I thought— I thought you were dead," he said weakly, but the head guardsman just smiled at him. "I could say the same for you. I saw that beast swallow you whole." He kneeled beside Pin and helped to sit his head up so Alyssia could help him drink the potion. "How did you get out?"

"I—" he took in a sharp breath from the pain of being moved. "I took a Magic Bomb from the shop before we left and kept it in my pouch," he said. "I set it off inside the monster's stomach and used a basic protection spell to shield myself. It wasn't very good, but... it kept me from dying."

Eldridge had seen the kind of damage those devices could do firsthand. It was a wonder he wasn't blown apart. "You took a bomb like that from close range?" There was a look of pride on Eldridge's face, and he brought his fist down lightly against Pin's shoulder. "'Atta boy."

With each gulp of the healing elixir, Pin's legs started to mend themselves. His bones shifted and contorted back into their original place. Torn muscle and ripped skin almost appeared to reverse in time and reform over the newly repaired bone.

"You would've been proud of him, you know," Alyssia said as she helped him drink the last of the healing potions. "He saved me from a demon just before you guys came."

"Of course he did," Eldridge said. "I would expect nothing less from a guardsman." He looked back to Pin. "Pin, I know you learned combat magic out of necessity for Green Haven, but... I don't think any of us will disagree with calling you a mage now."

Tears were swelling in Pin's eyes, even though he tried to hide them. "Thanks, Eldridge..." With a potion and a half in his system, he started to feel better a lot quicker. "So what do we do now? Are we really going to try to take on all those demons out there *and* Nahath? Just the four of us?" Pin asked.

It was then that Gorgron finally came over and placed the bag of potions on the ground. "The Wise One has blessed us with everything we need to stop the demons."

"Heh, good point," Eldridge said as he got to his feet. "We'll split the potions up evenly among us. Is this all we have?"

"Oh! Actually!" Alyssia perked up and removed the potion of Cyclops Strength from her pocket and sat it next to the bag. "I almost forgot about this."

Pin paused and looked legitimately puzzled for a moment. "Wait..." he said, closing his eyes and rubbing his forehead. He was trying to remember their previous interaction at his shop. "Alyssia. Didn't you use that? Did I sell you two of them? I can't remember..."

She raised an eyebrow at him. "What are you talking about?"

"I just saw you lift all of that rubble off of me. How did you do that without Cyclops Strength?" Pin asked, looking inquisitive.

"Huh? Oh. I— I don't know. I guess I'm just stronger than I thought I was?" she said. "You know Thorne always said I was pretty strong for an elf. Guess I never really tested it before now."

Despite her response, Pin still looked baffled. "I know you're pretty strong, but... that— that thing weighed like a ton. And I've never even seen you do a single push-up since I've known you." While Pin wouldn't pretend to know anything about basic elf biology, they generally were more known for their magic than their strength.

Alyssia frowned at that. "Pin, c'mon. Is it really the time for that right now? With everything going on, you're going to dwell on this?" The elf said, her voice sounding more annoyed.

It was then that Pin's resolve about the matter would shrink along with his stature. He wouldn't give a retort, but Gorgron stepped up closer to Alyssia and placed a strong hand on her shoulder. "Alyssia, it is time," he said in a calm voice.

Immediately, Alyssia grimaced, and she swatted his hand away. "Excuse me? Time for what?" She replied, taking a step back from him and, thus the rest of the group.

In contrast, Pin put his hands up in a surrendering position. "Hey, guys, this is my fault. I shouldn't have said anything."

Eldridge narrowed his eyes and took a glance at the orc and then Alyssia. "No. Let him speak. Gorgron, what is it time for?"

"The truth," he responded bluntly, his eyes staying focused on Alyssia. He had an unwavering stare. The same stare that he gave her at the bar when they first met. It sent chills down her spine just as it did then too. "The truth about *what*?" she said, giving him a confused look. "You're just saying a bunch of nonsense like you always do," she said.

Gorgron's features shifted into a frown from hearing her words. His voice had a layer of disappointment. "I *over*estimated you," the orc said as he turned toward Eldridge and Pin.

"She is constantly using a combination of transmutation and illusionary magic on herself."

Eldridge would give a glance at Pin as the boy was more well verse in magic than himself, but the only thing the mage could offer was a bewildered shrug in return. Pin understood the words but didn't fully understand what he was attempting to convey. "I don't get it. What are you trying to say, that she's changing her appearance?" Pin asked.

"Correct. That is not her true appearance."

"*Huh!?*" Pin blurted out. Eldridge, as the only person there who wasn't a magic user, looked utterly lost. But their reactions did not stop Gorgron from turning back to the red elf and speaking again.

"I don't care what you do after tonight, but that magic is draining you. You're only *half* as strong as you should be." Gorgron noticed her eyes start to dart around the room as she backed up into the kitchen counter.

Her natural response was to... laugh. Awkwardly. It sounded so fake that even she found it hard to believe. "Come on guys, you going to listen to this? This guys a lunatic, remember?"

CHAPTER FOUR

The room was silent for several moments as glances between the group were exchanged back and forth. Pin would break the silence first, "Alysia...? What's going on? What is he talking about?"

She couldn't even stand to make clear eye contact with him. She started to chew on her bottom lip.

Gorgron stepped forward again. "You told me you wanted to help these people." The orc's frustration was starting to show. He bared his teeth, finally allowing some of his race's more primal instincts to seep through. "Or do you prefer to stand back *again* and let more children die in front of you?"

Alyssia practically felt her heart drop into her stomach. She closed her eyes tightly. She heard the sounds of screaming all around them as the monsters raided the town. Her gaze fell toward Pin, who looked the most confused at the whole situation, and tears started to roll down her cheeks. "I'm sorry, Pin..."

Her hands began to glow mythically, with the elf waving them back and forth in an odd pattern. In Pin and Eldridge's mind, it was out of character for her. They hadn't ever seen her use magic before.

It would take a few seconds, but with the final wave of her hand, there was like a haze was slowly being lifted from around her. The image of a red-skinned elf was dissipating, and in its place stood something that did not look remotely like the form they originally witnessed her to be. She looked more like a template of what a bipedal humanoid should look like. She had hair but no eyebrows or nose. She had a mouth with no lips. There were no wrinkles, veins, or any distinguishable characteristics that made up a regular person.

Her form looked as if someone was instructed on how to draw a human or an elf without having ever actually seen one. From there, her frame began to twist, deform and reshape. Parts of her body were suddenly bulging out and expanding. Thick fur started to coat over her like a canine while her face freakishly extended to a snout that was similar to a hyena's.

Her back raised, her spine shifted out and developed into a severe hunchback that forced her posture forward to the point that her new, large gorilla-like arms were almost to the ground. She stood up on hind legs that were similar to a feline's. Instead of feet, she had large paws that held up her form. Her fur was the same color of red that her skin was before.

"Good Lord..." Eldridge uttered under his breath. His eyes stretched open wide at the sight of the creature in front of him. He glanced over to Pin, who's mouth had dropped open in sheer disbelief at what he was seeing. "Yo-you're a demon!?" Pin shouted.

Despite how she looked, Alyssia tried and failed to appear as small as possible in front of them. "*I'm not a demon!*" She pleaded. "I mean— not— not *technically*! Not exactly—!" Her words were coming out frantic.

Gorgron interrupted her babbling. "This is her *actual* cursed form," he explained. "What you were seeing before was just a fabrication she made up with magic."

"It's... true," Alyssia said. "With magic, I was able to get close to what I looked like before, but—"

"Explain it to them later." The orc said abruptly, as he headed toward the door. "Or there won't be a town left to save."

"And where are you going?" Eldridge said.

"To find Nahath and kill him." He glanced back at the group. "Use your potions to protect the people still alive. I don't need them." And with that, the orc left the house as swiftly as he had arrived, leaving just the three of them there. They all shared awkward glances with one another. Alyssia spoke first.

"I don't— I don't think I need them either," Alyssia said as she looked down at her hands. They looked more like claws or talons with sharp, piercing nails. She felt good. Better than she had felt in a long time. It had been so long that she had forgotten how much of a toll the constant use of magic had on her body. To keep that kind of magic up day in and day out was exhausting, and it was only much more evident to her now. Her field of view stayed toward the floor, though. She didn't even want to look at the horror that was on their faces. She could already feel the eyes of the two burrowing into her.

And she wasn't wrong. Eldridge and Pin could only stare at the grotesqueness of her true form. But one thing was for certain: Gorgron was right. They didn't have much time to put a stop to this. Eldridge cleared his throat and spoke.

"Alyssia," Eldridge said in a firm voice that appeared to visibly startle her and cause her eyes to shift up from the ground. "Are you saying you are really able to kill those monsters without any aid? Just bare handed?"

Slowly, she nodded her head. "I think so. With the way I feel now? I—uh... feel pretty confident." She was surprised about how right Gorgron was about her. She felt like she could lift twice the amount she did before.

"Good," Eldridge affirmed. "I assume since these things eat us, they are going to be attracted to the largest congregation of people." Eldridge reached for his helmet that was on the ground and put it on but did not yet pull down the face plate. "I leave the protection of Mace and Tulips to you. That seems fitting, no?"

Alyssia was shocked. This was the first time anyone had ever actually talked to her like a person without the use of her illusion spell. What appeared to be a smile spread across her canine features, and she nodded. "Y-yeah. Okay. You got it."

Eldridge then turned to Pin. "Pin. Give me something that will help me kill those things," he said. It took Pin a second or two to respond, but eventually, he snapped out of the trance-like state he was in. So many things had happened tonight that it felt like his brain was still trying to catch up. "Right. Yeah." He crouched down to take a look into the potion bag. "The limit a normal person should take at once without killing their organs is three." He dug through the bag and brought out a few of the useful ones that were still left and offered it to Eldridge. "Here. Cyclop's Strength, Golem Skin, and a potion of speed. They'll have a hard time killing you with these three."

Eldridge grinned. "Speed, endurance, and strength. I like it." He took the potions from him and started to drink them all one by one. Pin spoke up. "They're not forever. You will have the effects for about twenty minutes," Pin said. It was then that he felt embarrassed about his own shortcomings as a potion maker. Some of these would normally last an hour or longer when made by a skilled artisan that knew how to weave the ingredients properly. Eldridge may or may not have known this fact, but Pin saw him simply smile and shut his face plate after drinking. "Perfect," he said. "I shouldn't need longer than that. But do you have any more still at the shop?"

"Uh. I don't know. Maybe there might be one or two in a drawer somewhere—"

"Get them," Eldridge said as he picked up his lance. "Gorgron shared something with me in the forest." He looked between the two of them. It was at this very moment that he realized they were all the people of this town had left if they hoped to see the next day. "There is a barrier deep into the forest that's blocking exit and entry. There won't be any cavalry. And evacuation is meaningless. We stop Nahath now, or we all die here." Eldridge's tone was deadly serious, and Pin and Alyssia nodded their heads as he moved to the door.

Pin swallowed nervously at the news, but Alyssia's aura was surprisingly calm. She had resolved to stay to fight for Green Haven. There being a barrier didn't change that.

Pin went to grab the bag with the remaining potions inside.

Eldridge spoke, "I'm going to try to save as many people as I can while I attempt to find Sarah and Molly. We'll meet back at Mace and Tulips in around fifteen minutes. Understood?" He took a glance around to make sure the two had no objections to his orders. No one protested. "Alright then. Let's go!" Eldridge and Pin ran out the door first, with both of them running off in different directions.

Alyssia stayed behind. She took just a second to take a deep inhale and a long exhale. "Come on, Alyssia. You can do this. Come on... Come on."

Since she had been cursed, the only thing she could think about was how to get back to her old body. But until tonight, she had never considered the advantages of her new one. She crouched down, using her powerful digitigrade feline-like legs as a spring so she could jump onto the rooftop of a nearby house through the hole in the ceiling the worm demon had made. Her landing was a little shaky at first, but she was able to reorient herself. *Wow. I can't believe I just did that,* she thought. Then she jumped to another rooftop. And another. And another. Soon she was moving fast. So fast that she cleared entire blocks in a fraction of the time it would have taken her before.

It was ironic that after all this time of working with Thorne, tonight was the first time she was in a rush to get to work.

Chapter Five

After leaving the house, Gorgron headed straight for the town hall. Now that the demons were here and Nahath had revealed his true self, he could sense where the dark presence he felt earlier was. Demons that tried to interrupt his progress were quickly dealt with. A winged demonic beast swooped down to grab him, but the orc raised his hand and grabbed its leg first. Its body appeared to shrivel up and become sickly almost immediately. It lost whatever color it had before inevitably falling limp to the ground, struggling to breathe.

Most other demons were dealt with in the same way. The orc used his magic to kill and destroy any and every creature in his way until he found himself in front of the entrance to the town hall. Sensing demonic energy from within, he opened the doors and walked straight to the mayor's office. Upon entering, he discovered there was no one there. At least, not in view. While the mayor had done a good job of sealing it away before, the smell of demons and undead was far too much to mask from the orc now. "Where are you?" the orc growled to himself, practically tearing the room apart in search of some clue as to where the mayor went. In a rage, he flipped over the desk in the office, which revealed a trap door beneath it. It was secure with a heavy padlock, but the orc had more than enough strength to rip the metal apart and brute force his way into opening the door.

The trap door led down to what appeared to be an underground basement with a long stretch of stairs that almost disappear into the near pitch-black darkness below. Without hesitation, Gorgron made his way down the stone stairs, each step causing a loud echo to bounce back to his ears. The staircase led him to a barely lit room, only illuminated by a few candles.

He had to focus his eyes to see anything properly. There were numerous odd statues of demonic creatures that were scattered throughout the room. And at the other end of the basement stood Nahath with his back to Gorgron, standing over a simple wooden table. On the table was a wooden box with a key lying next to it.

The mayor turned his head to have a look at who was intruding. Even in the dark room, Gorgron could make out the man's face... or at least what was left of it. The left half of his face looked to have been severely burned, with the charred fleshed having been scrapped off from the bone. His left eye was still in its socket, but it was black and burned, with no eyelid to conceal it. The other half of his face was not untouched. He had a few third-degree burns there as well, with flesh starting to peel. The former mayor chuckled, half his features lifting into a grin when he saw Gorgron. "You just continue to impress, don't you? Hard to believe you survived that long in a forest full of demons without any supplies."

The mayor's face was such a far cry from what the orc had seen before. Any normal human would have been bed ridden from such horrible burns. "The Wise One supplies all the nourishment I need," he said.

Nahath's chuckle turned into full-blown laughter. He laughed hard and loud. The sound of his voice echoed throughout the basement. "You mean your *fake god?*" he said between breaths. "No one has *ever* heard of him. You're just a magic user. An advanced one, sure, but there's nothing 'spiritual' about what you do."

Nahath couldn't help but find the absurdity of the situation hilarious. Gorgron was silent for a moment before speaking.

"Was this your plan? To sit here and hide in your cellar while you let those demons consume your people?" It was only after those words that Nahath's laughter finally died. There were a few moments of pause before he raised his head and spread his arms out to their full length as if admiring the handiwork of the place they were standing in. "Do you like it? I had the carpenters build this place under the guise that it would be used as some kind of bunker. A final hold out for the town if the invading demons became too much. It's kind of ironic looking back now, isn't it?"

"You're a coward," Gorgron said. He took a couple steps forward but suddenly lost his balance and almost fell when it felt like his foot had sunk down into the floor itself. When he looked down at the ground, he saw a large set of bright red eyes embedded into the floor staring back up at him. He saw that part of the stone floor had parted into a gaping maw that had trapped his foot inside. Whatever demon this was, he could feel its sharp teeth bearing down on his ankle and trapping him where he was.

"You think I *want* to do this?" Nahath replied, moving over closer to the stuck orc but not so close that he would be within arm's reach of him. Gorgron bared his teeth, growling. Behind him, one of the statues in the room came to life. A tall and lanky bear-like creature with long arms grabbed onto the orc to further restrain him. Instead of paws, it had hands akin to that of a human. It grabbed Gorgron's wrists to keep him from touching anything.

"Let me show you something, Gorgron." the former mayor reached down to his forearm and dug his fingers into the flesh there. He proceeded to rip skin and muscle fibers from the bone as if it was nothing. Veins were ripped out until they broke, splattering blood all over the floor. "Do you see this? I don't even *feel* it."

He then proceeded to unclasp and undo the chest piece of his armor, letting it drop to the floor. He lifted his shirt soon after, revealing a large hole that was in the center of his chest. Where one would have expected to see red blood and pink organs inside, in actuality, was just a rotted-out void instead. Blood had long since dried with innards that looked dry and blackened. Like a flower that had long since decayed.

There was no life inside of him. At least nothing that anyone would recognize traditionally as being alive.

"Look at me, orc. I haven't been 'the mayor' in years. I'm just a limp, rotting corpse held together by magic and my master's whims." Nahath pulled his shirt back down and turned his back to Gorgron so he could focus his attention on the wooden box that sat on the table.

"You know... I found out firsthand just how much these demons love the taste of human flesh. The joy on my master's face as they ate my heart in front of me, was the last thing I saw before I died."

Gorgron tried to fight against the demons binding him, but he could do very little to force his way out of their grasp, physically. "Who did this to you, Nahath?" he said. "Who is this 'master'?"

"Does it matter now?" Nahath's hand appeared to rub over the wood and metal material of the wooden box almost lovingly. "I'm just a puppet, that's so close to cutting his strings..." He looked back at the orc as the rest of the statues in the room came alive. Other weird, grotesque abominations, seemingly having life breathed into them anew. "Do you even know how these demons work? The smart ones will use human souls as batteries," he explained. "They devour us to sustain their physical forms, lest they would eventually rot away and get dragged back into hell..." As he spoke, Nahath opened the wooden chest in front of him. There was a severed eye inside with a thin yellow slit in the middle that looked akin to a pupil. It was too big to be a human eye, and the anatomy was wrong. Only the top of the eye and the bottom had severed nerves that connected it to the brain. There was none behind it.

"Is that... the eye of a demon?" Gorgron said.

"Yes. But it's not *just* an eye..." as Nahath spoke in reply, there were ghastly figures that appeared to melt through the walls. The odd manifestations wailed, appearing to be drawn to the eye itself before eventually being absorbed into it. The manifestations had human faces that were twisted, horrified versions of the citizens above. "With the right magic, the eye of a demon can be used as a means of attracting and absorbing human souls." Nahath took a moment to stare at the eye, almost as if admiring it, before gently grabbing the optic orb and lifting it out of the box.

"You see, once my master finds out I've been straying too far out of line, they'll remove their magic from me... and once that happens, I'll experience what *'real death'* is like. But with this... I won't need their magic anymore," he said.

"So you're going to use your own people as fuel to keep your rotting corpse alive?" Gorgron looked disgusted. His ankle was starting to bleed from the demon biting into him, but that did little more than to further ignite his anger.

Nahath simply smiled at the orc. Or at least as best as he could, considering the severe damage to his face. "I must look so cruel to an outsider like you," he said. "But what I do is a blessing compared to what my master had in store for this town. The only thing I regret is what I had to do to the guardsmen. The twisted and horrified looks on their faces, are going to haunt me for the rest of my existence." He tilts his head back, holding the demon's eyeball over his mouth. It looked as if he was about to eat it. "Eldridge and Pin especially..."

"You underestimated them," Gorgron said bluntly as he struggled against the demons that held him. "Neither of them are dead." When those words left Gorgron's mouth, Nahath looked shocked for a moment and paused. But then, he appeared to be rather cheerful. "I'm glad." he said as he held the eye over his mouth, which stretched open to the point that his jaw unhinged. He swallowed it whole with an audible gulp. The souls that were so drawn to the eye continued to fill the room, giving a haunting wail as their ghostly forms disappeared into Nahath's body. He closed his eyes and let out a content sigh as if experiencing a breath of air for the first time.

"Do you have any idea what it's like to be murdered and then brought back as a husk of your former self?"

Nahath proceeded to kneel on the cold stone floor as he beckoned something over to him. A small, gray creature akin to an imp looked to almost phase through the wall in order to get to the former mayor. Its red eyes pierced through the darkness of the room, and Nahath took a knife from his pocket and grabbed the little creature's arm. He proceeded to cut its wrist, but it didn't even flinch as thick ink-like blobs of blood drained onto the floor below. With his finger, Nahath began to draw symbols with the blood as if using it as ink. "No taste, no smell. I pretend to eat in front of people just so I can vomit it back up later." The blood began to glow a yellow color.

Traces from the symbol that was on the ground started to spread to other parts of the floor, appearing to weave through cracks. It was now that Gorgron took notice of other symbols around the basement. Dried blood markings once concealed by magic, now all appearing and illuminating at once. "You've been such a nuisance to me, Gorgron," Nahath said as he then stood up. The room became more visible, going from near pitch black to a glowing, bright yellow. "I thought that maybe sending you out to the forest to die would have gotten rid of you, but I'm glad you're alive to witness what happens next."

The orc spoke in response, "Yes. But you won't be." It was then that he closed his eyes and started to mutter a prayer.

Nahath laughed. "And what? You think praying to 'The Wise One' will save you?"

When the orc opened his eyes again, he proceeded to turn his head to the point that his neck started to strain to look back. There was a loud crack heard as his head turned all the way around with his chin facing where his back was. Gorgron opened his mouth, and a kind of burning green fire was unleashed from the orifice upon the bear demon that was holding him. The creature screamed from the flames and was quickly burned to ashes.

The one eye that Nahath had opened wide in surprise. "Are you... Are you the living dead as well?"

There was a sound of squishing and cracking as the muscle and bones in Gorgron's neck twisted back into place. "I am whatever The Wise One wills me to be."

"It is just so funny to me that you actually think *gods* care about what happens to us."

Nahath placed his hand on the ground. "I'm going to show you how pathetic those powers your fake god has given you compared to the REAL power that I have now."

Chapter Six

Am I— am I really doing this? Alyssia thought as her sharp talons were used to rip through a winged demon that was on top of one of the roofs. She didn't even recognize herself. Or the loud and carnivorous-like roar that came from her maw when another flying demon penetrated her shoulder with its tube-like stinger. Her talons sunk into its skull, and when she ripped off part of its head, it let out a noise akin to a yelp before flopping down harmlessly and tumbling to the ground. It surprised her just how easy it was to kill the demon fodder. She felt stronger now than she ever had. She was never much of a fighter, but the physiology of this cursed form of hers made it feel as natural as breathing. She left piles of dismembered demons in her wake, her fur becoming stained in blood.

She tried her best not to let anyone see her on the way to Mace and Tulips, but sometimes it was unavoidable. Every so often, she had to save the townsfolk from a demon or keep one from breaking into a home. Their reaction to her appearance was what she had come to expect without having her magic activated. Shrieks of horror, paralyzation from fear, running away. All expected, but reactions that she wasn't accustomed to anymore.

It hardly mattered at this point, though. She was only concerned about saving as many people as she could. And there were a lot of them to save. There were so many demons between her and the inn that she had lost track of where she was supposed to be going. It was only when she heard the loud sound of a gunshot that her concentration came back into focus. She wasn't a gun expert, but she knew the sound of a blunderbuss being fired when she heard one. *Thorne!* She thought before she immediately started to run toward Mace and Tulips. At first, she ran on two legs like she always did, but then, gradually and naturally, she eased down onto her claws and began to run on all fours. It... almost made her feel uneasy with how natural running like this felt. It was almost as subconscious as tying her shoes.

As she made her way closer, she heard Thorne's voice. It was coming from inside the inn, so it was muffled, but she recognized his dwarven tongue from anywhere. "Keep 'em at bay, lads! Don' let 'em in!" His yells were followed by another gun shot being fired. By the time she got there, it was a horrific sight outside of the bar. There were splatters of blood everywhere on the ground, but instead of seeing bodies, there were just dismembered limbs and body parts that looked to have been chewed or bitten off. Dozens of demons were crowded at the door. They appeared to be the shape of large eyeballs that were each as big as a full adult human. Blood continuously dripped off of them as if they had just been ripped out of an eye socket. They floated in mid-air, defying the need for gravity. Parts of the double doors to the inn were broken off which created gaps that the demons could use to squeeze inside. She heard multiple gun shots coming from the inn now, but even as the monsters took several bullets, they hardly appeared to slow down at all.

On the side of Mace and Tulips, she noticed someone trying to escape by opening one of the bedroom windows from the second floor. It was a woman who then proceeded to jump out of the open window in desperation. When she fell to the ground, she must've landed on her leg wrong as she let out a loud scream in pain and collapsed. The sound of the scream immediately alerted the floating eyes, who all shifted focus and instead headed to where they heard the cry.

Upon seeing this, Alyssia immediately sprinted into action, using all

CHAPTER SIX

four of her limbs to gather as much speed and momentum as she could. But the demons were fast. Even faster than she was. Three of them made their way around the building in no time. She watched the bottom half of the three eyeballs split open and separate, revealing a mouth that was hidden underneath. They had sharp-looking fanged teeth, and their maw leaked saliva profusely. Each of the three eye demons took a bite out of the woman, resulting in an ear-piercing scream. Alyssia made it over in time to grab one of the creatures off of her, digging her claws into it in anger right before using her strength to crush the eyeball into paste. Trying to get the other two off of her was like trying to force a rapid dog to unclench its jaws.

She tore the eyeballs asunder, but not before one had managed to take a large bite out of the woman's torso, which caused her to start convulsing on the ground. The smell of fresh blood in the air made the other demons just as rabid as they made their way from around the corner. The demons, dozens of them, all began to pile on top of the woman, ignoring Alyssia's presence completely. It was almost like they were in a trance, obsessed with the taste of mortal flesh.

She tried with everything within her to stop the demons, but even as she ripped into some of them, the others simply ignored her in favor of their meal. The only thing more haunting than the woman's agonizing screams was the sickening crunch of bone and the squishing of muscle and flesh between the monster's teeth when they bit off chunks of her.

The next few seconds were all it took for the screaming to stop and the woman to get devoured in front of her eyes. In that short span of time, she became unrecognizable. Just a pile of meat and severed bone that was a disgrace to have even called a person. Sadness overtook Alyssia, and then rage came next. She partly blamed herself. She was right next to the woman, but could do little but watch her be eaten by these monstrosities.

She became so angry that she partially blacked out. She didn't remember much of what happened after that. She threw every bit of caution to the wind and proceeded to bare her teeth like a feral animal. She started to rip, bite, and claw her way through the legion of eye demons. Now that their meal was finished, they retaliated this time. Biting into her with their sharp teeth and strong jaws. Her skin was much harder to penetrate than the woman's, but they were still able to rip chunks of flesh out of her eventually. Any pain she felt, she ignored. Adrenaline took over for several long minutes until her heart was pounding through her chest. She didn't stop until her claws and teeth had torn through every single one of them.

Eventually, after killing all of them, the cursed elf finally found herself slumped up against the side of the inn, out of breath and panting. Seconds later, she would lose consciousness.

The next thing she remembered was hearing Thorne's voice. "'Ey, lass! Lass! Stay wit' me, lass!" When Alyssia finally comes to, the first face she saw was Thone's. He'd knelt down beside her, keeping her head held up to make it easier for her to breathe. "Thorne?" She said weakly before wincing. Consciousness and lack of adrenaline made her now aware of the numerous bites all over her body. Some were more severe, with pieces of flesh having been bit off from her arms, legs, and torso. "Easy, lass, easy. Those things took a few chunks outta ya." He gave her a smile and then a laugh. "But ya tore through 'em! We just had ta' clear out da stragglers!" After he said that, it was then that she became aware of the other people who were there now. They all had these frightened looks on their faces. Some had guns and knives, while others had last-minute makeshift weaponry like broken beer bottles or pitch forks. Every single one of them looked confused. She wondered what they were all staring at. Were her wounds really that bad?

It was the realization that her illusion spell wasn't up that caused her eyes to snap open and her to scramble. She tried quickly to get up, but she was held down by Thorne, even as she struggled against him. "Alyssia, stop!" he yelled. "Ya're gonna bleed out!" She hadn't even realized that the hand she couldn't see of Thorne's had a towel in it that was covered in blood and pressed firmly against a deep wound at her side. She struggled more against him, but dwarfs were surprisingly strong for their size. And at her angle, it was hard to get leverage without potentially hurting him. "Oh god, Thorne. Thorne! They're gonna see me!" She managed to get to a sitting position to try to get up, but by that point, the dwarf had wrapped his arms around her torso to keep her where she was. "They already have, lass!" the dwarf said, managing to keep her in place. "They already have..." his voice got softer in tone, and the obvious realization had hit her all at once.

She seen the horrid looks on the people's faces. A few took a step back when they saw that she was sitting up now. Tears that she had no hope to contain formed in her eyes. They heard her voice. They heard Thorne call her Alyssia. Her life in Green Haven was over now. When she looked over at Thorne, the look of compassion and empathy that was on his face was in complete contrast to the others. It was a look that she wasn't used to seeing on him. In fact, she didn't even know it was a look he was capable of. Her voice started to break from the tears that were actively falling down her cheek now. "Thorne... how did you know it was me?"

Thorne didn't answer at first. Instead he chose to take her claw to help him apply pressure to the wound at her side. "I was a cleric fa' well over two decades, lass," the dwarf said, giving her clawed hand a few pats to comfort her. "I've always known. Takes a wee bit more than a few spells ta' trick these old eyes."

By that point, any composure Alyssia had was gone. She buried her head into Thorne's shoulder and started to bawl. "I'm sorry, Thorne! I'm sorry..." Thorne gives her a pat and a rub on the back. "Aye, aye! Ain't the first ta' try ta' hide their true face from me. Should'ta seen me ex-wife without 'er makeup on." He gave a hearty laugh, but she just smiled against his shoulder. Same old Thorne.

By that point, the whispers from the townspeople were becoming more audible. It was hard for her not to overhear it.

"Is that really, Alyssia?"

"Did they turn her into a monster?"

"What the hell is she?"

"Don't get near her."

A few of the men in the group slowly inched their way forward. All of them had their weapons clinched firmly in their hands. One of them spoke. "Thorne, we can't stay out here. We gotta get back inside."

Thorne nodded. "Agreed. C'mon, help me get 'er inside."

His request was only met with silence and a few awkward glances. "Thorne, you can't be serious," the man said. "Those monsters have been slaughtering us left and right, and you want to bring one inside with us? My *kids* are in there." It was obvious that the rest of the group shared the man's perspective as a few other men came forth beside him in agreement, still holding their weaponry.

Thorne frowned deeply. "She's one o' our own!" Thorne retaliated. "I don' care what she looks like. She's comin' inside wit' us!"

Another man became frantic and drew his rifle, aiming down the barrel's sights at the two of them. "You're not bringing that THING inside with us!" Not long after he spoke those words, others voiced their grievances as well.

"If you love it so much, *you* stay out here with it."

"Yeah!"

"Keep that monster out of the inn!"

There was a thick air of silence that befell around Thorne. And then, he began to reach for the blunderbuss that was on the ground next to him. "Afta' everything I've done for ya, ya gonna kick me outta me own business?" With a swift motion, he had the end of the barrel pointed toward the group, which took many aback. "Well, if ya want ta' take over me inn, ya could pry it from me cold dead hands, ya bampots!"

It was at this point that Alyssia stepped in and lowered the barrel of the blunderbuss gun. "Everyone, just stop!" Alyssia shouted. "I'm not coming inside." She turns to Thorne before speaking, "Thorne, thank you. Really. But I'm fine. I'll be okay."

She could tell by the look on his face that he didn't believe her. To prove it, she started the painful process of getting up to her feet. Thorne was right that any normal person would be about to bleed out with the amount of blood that she lost, but the body she was cursed with was far more resilient than that. She still clutched at her side in pain, but she wasn't in danger of dying. At least not yet. "See?"

Thorne started to speak, but he noticed that the ground below him began to illuminate with bright lines of yellow. One line connected to another, and then another, and another. This process repeated as if they were working together to form some kind of image or outline of something. The townspeople tried to avoid stepping on any of them, but it became an inevitability once the stone streets steadily became covered in them. It was like the town had become infected, as even the buildings were coated in the odd lines and symbols.

"What... what *is* this?" Alyssia asked, only being able to stare in awe with both horror and amazement.

"S'been so long since I laid me eyes on one, but... this is a Summonin' Circle..." Thorne said, getting to his feet as well. "But it's da biggest I've seen. It's like it's engulfin' da whole town."

Alyssia looked confused for a second. "I'm sorry. *A what?*"

Thorne sucks his teeth at her ignorance on the subject. For her age, he expected her to know more about the basics of magic. "It's in da *name*, lass," he said plainly. "It's used ta summon creatures. Usually from otha' realms."

It was only after the end of his sentence that the realization hit Alyssia. "That's how Nahath has been summoning demons here..." Alyssia said, mostly to herself, but Thorne overheard it.

"Nahath's been doin' *what!?*" Thorne said, his confusion only being matched by the sound of his rising anger.

"I'll tell you later! Just tell me how do we stop it!?" she said. Her heart felt like it sank when she saw Thorne just shake his head.

"It's alreadae started, child. None o' us can staph it now."

Eldridge sprinted at full speed through Green Haven. He ran faster than he ever has, even without full armor on. The way he practically glided when he ran was unlike anything he had ever experienced. He had always viewed the practice of magic as being something unnatural, but now, he was finally starting to understand the appeal. With the speed potion, he felt faster than the wind itself, despite the fact that he was still wearing full plate armor. It would have taken ten or fifteen minutes to cover the distance of what he did in a minute now.

Most demons were too slow to even keep up with him. He speared through them with his lance like nothing. The Cyclops Strength potion made him strong enough to the point that the once heavy lance was as light as a feather now. He wielded it as if it was a mere extension of his arm. He had never felt so powerful, but he knew these powers wouldn't stay. He was on borrowed time and had to get home quickly.

And thus, there was no moment wasted for pleasantries or explanations when he saved someone from a demon. One moment he was there, with his spear through a hideous beast's head, and the next moment, he was gone.

Before long, he would arrive at his house, but he didn't bother to open the door normally. With his newfound strength, he slammed through the entrance like nothing. "Sarah! Molly!" he yelled at the top of his lungs. There was no direct answer in the house. There wasn't even a lantern lit. With it being nightfall now, the house was almost completely dark, but it wasn't silent. Within the darkness was the faint sound of something being chewed. Like meat being torn from bone.

CHAPTER SIX

The sound alone made his stomach churn. He gripped his lance tightly while he made his way through the house and felt around in the dark with his free hand for a lantern. He remembered there being one on the kitchen counter. Shockingly, it was still there. He lit the lantern and soon afterward was venturing into his home as if it was the first time. Thankfully the house wasn't terribly large. Down the end of the hall was the master bedroom where he and his wife slept. Every creak of the floorboard was just as loud in his ears as the eating that was occurring on the other side of the room's door.

The door was partially opened, and the sounds of a feast were deafening. He could hear each and every one of his own breaths while his heart was now pounding through his chest.

He gripped the doorknob and took a moment to steel himself for the worst before swinging open the door. In the room, there looked to be four citizens from town. He remembers their faces. One was a baker, another a gardener. He forgot the professions of the other two, but there had to have been at least seven dead bodies lying in the room that the four citizens were actively cannibalizing. Each of the seven bodies were in a different state, and only one of them had a face that was distinguishable. The others had limbs torn off, with their arms and legs almost completely eaten clean to the bone. The amount of scattered meat and limbs tossed around carelessly was a scene he was more used to seeing in a butcher shop. The fact that it was happening in his own home made him reel back, on the verge of vomiting.

He couldn't tell if the bodies were Sarah's or Molly's, and the horror of not knowing made him petrified. He couldn't move. He couldn't attack. It was as if his brain was in a fog. The light of his lantern caught the attention of one of them: the townsperson, seemingly devoid of any coherent thought, looked at the knight and gave a loud hiss through her blood-soaked teeth.

He was taken aback. Enough so that he almost tripped when stepping back in his heavy armor. He had heard of situations like this before. Demonic Possession. A normal person sharing their body unwillingly with the spirit of a demon. He wasn't sure if the demons were fully in control of them or had just given them an unquenchable appetite, but he had no idea what to do with these people. The woman who had hissed before simply went back to eating. They were like a herd of lions that were feasting off of a fresh kill. Why even try to pursue him when they already had several meals in front of them?

Few priests and holy people in town could address a phenomenon like this. But they probably weren't even alive by this point. He felt powerless as he simply stood there and watched them consume the dead bodies of townspeople who had undoubtedly been murdered by the four of them.

It was then that, out of the corner of his eye, he saw one of them pick something up and wipe their blood-covered lips with it. They were using a garment of some kind and Eldridge shined the lantern's light in the room to get a better look. What he saw was one of his daughter's dresses coated in blood.

Something in Eldridge broke at that exact moment. He forgot his oath to protect, he forgot about his plans to meet up with the others at the inn, and he forgot about the other citizens in need. His body moved before his brain could fully process the complex array of emotions he was feeling.

He gripped his lance as hard as he could and speared it through the side of one of the possessed citizen's faces. For a second, the other three townspeople looked surprised at the action. A sign that some humanity was still left somewhere in their subconsciousness. But this was only for a moment. In the next moment, one of them rushed at the knight, giving out a roar that was more akin to a wild beast than any human he had ever heard. He slammed the side of his fully armored fist into the citizen's head, not realizing just how much force he was exerting from his newfound strength.

The man's skull shattered the moment Eldridge's fist connected, and

CHAPTER SIX

he fell to the ground, lifeless, his body giving a spasming twitch every so often. Another one of the Possessed came up to throw a punch at Eldridge's armor, but it did very little but break the bones in their hand. It only took a swift, crushing elbow to shatter their collarbone. He would find that there were even more of these Possessed people in his home. Hidden in closets or other rooms. They all came at him at once in different directions, hissing, some even growling, demonically. At one point, he dropped the lantern he was holding, his vision completely black now as he was overwhelmed by the demon-possessed people.

Without hesitation this time, Eldridge began to put them down one by one. Punching, kicking, head-butting. There was no honor or technique to what he did here. Just a savage brute swinging wildly with murderous intent. Later on, he would probably reflect back to the people who originally trained him to be a knight. How disappointed they would have been with this barbaric display of him murdering citizens like some kind of primitive animal.

Blood covered the walls with numerous bodies slumped on the floor all around him, and when he was finally done, the guardsman dropped to his knees, panting for breath. His mind was flooded with thoughts. This was his family's home. Him and his wife had their first child here. The memories of Molly's first steps flashed into his mind as well as the first time he had to wake up in the middle of the night to rock her. Tears poured from his eyes, and he took off his helmet so he could breathe easier. It occurred to him now that he hadn't even tried to save these people. He just maimed them like some kind of executioner.

He buried his face inside his gauntlets and wept openly. But, just a few moments later, he noticed that the house started to illuminate from little lines that began to connect and form shapes and symbols he had never seen before. They spread throughout the home like wildfire until it was covered in it. The once pitch-black house was now almost as bright as it was during the middle of a sunny day.

"Nahath... what have you done."

Pin was terrified after separating from the group. Demons were everywhere, and casting magic was no easy feat for him still. Sure, he could probably burn several of the demons with fire magic, but eventually, they were going to overwhelm him. His fears had led him to hide inside an old, rusty hay wagon. He covered himself and the bag of potions in hay so he wouldn't be noticed by any of the monsters that were wandering about. He had been brave a few times before, but now the realization of everything that was happening was finally catching up to him. He lay still in the wagon, crying at his cowardice. He covered his ears to muffle the sound of the cries for help as well as the hisses and roars of the demons around him.

He couldn't do this. Just yesterday, he was a potion maker, and now he was expected to fend off legions of demons on his own? He was absolutely frozen in fear. He did well to steady his breathing in a way that he escaped the notice of most of the demons that wandered by. There wasn't anything resembling a real plan here. He figured he would just try to hide until morning or until he couldn't anymore. He had the thought that maybe Nahath would take his demon legion and leave once he was done with whatever he was planning. Or maybe Gorgron would kill him and return things back to normal.

Either way, he didn't want to move. This was the safest he had felt since before entering the forest, and he was not very willing to give up his hiding spot. Over time things around him grew quiet. The demons seemingly had moved on to another part of town. It was dead silence for a while, but then, there was an odd noise that cut through the stillness like a knife. It was the sound of... sniffing? Almost akin to that of a dog tracking down a scent. The noise got louder and then went further away. And then came back again. If he didn't know any better, he would have

CHAPTER SIX

thought it was a hound dog trying to track down a rabbit for its master.

He heard the sound go from several yards away to several feet away. It then started to circle the wagon he was in. As hard as it was, he did his best to lower his panicked breathing in spite of his fear.

Before long, the sniffing would stop, and dead silence returned. It was probably only for ten seconds or so, but it might as well have been an eternity. He held his breath, and his heart was beating so loud he heard it in his ears. Suddenly, he could feel the wagon start to tip over. Gravity took effect, and he toppled out of the wagon with all the hay that it was carrying. The mage landed on the ground next to the bag of potions and grunted in pain when his face connected to the cold stone of the road.

Not wasting time, he got his bearings rather quickly. He shifted to get to his feet, only for him to feel dwarfed immediately by the demon that had overturned the wagon. It was a tall creature that stood on two legs with claws on its hands and feet. Its face had small beady eyes that looked almost useless. Instead of a mouth, it had a long prehensile snout akin to that of an elephant's. Even now, it continued to sniff, its snout weaving back and forth before settling in Pin's direction.

Pin quickly ignited a fireball in his hand and blasted it at the wagon he was just in, causing it to burst into flame. The sudden feeling of heat caused the creature to cover its face and stumble back a couple times. It was enough of a distraction that it bought Pin time to run. He picked up the bag of potions and ran as fast as he could. He ran until he finally arrived at his original destination: his potion shop. Seconds later, he got inside and shut the door before engaging the lock. He dropped the bag and fell to his knees, trying to catch his breath. "I— I made it..." he said, between pants. Without a doubt, he knew he had run past a few demons on the way to the shop, so he peeked through the entrance door's window. Sure enough, there were a couple demons outside starting to gather and look around, but not knowing the direction he went in. At the very least, he was safe for the time being. He decided to spend some time looking around the shop, rummaging through a couple things here and there.

Without light, the shop was so dark that he could barely see. But he didn't dare light a lantern. The last thing he needed was to risk attracting the demons to where he was. As he searched for whatever potions he may have had left, there was a small whine that echoed through the darkness. And then a faint whisper. It wasn't loud. In fact, if he wasn't so on edge, he wouldn't have even noticed it. The sounds had come from a nearby closet. He gulped down his nerves audibly and started preparing his fire spell with his left hand as he crept toward the door. Every squeak of the floorboards from his footsteps rang loud in his ears as he placed his hand softly on the doorknob of the closet. He counted to three in his head and swung open the storage closet with his fireball spell ready to blast anything that was inside. But, instead of being met with a ferocious demon, he found a woman with long blonde hair clutching her child tightly. The daughter was clinging onto her mother just as tightly, but she wasn't able to stop herself from trembling. Pin stopped the spell immediately and kneeled down beside them. "Hey, hey. Don't worry, I'm not going to hurt you," he said.

Hearing a familiar voice, the woman turned to face him. Her face was covered in tears. "Pin?" she said curiously, almost not believing it was him.

Pin felt the overwhelming sense of dread and fear lift just a little from seeing a familiar face. "Sarah!?" Pin responded. The two of them had very few interactions with one another, but this was Eldridge's wife and his daughter, Molly. He was sure Eldridge was going to be thrilled to see them still alive. "Oh, man, Eldridge was so worried about you two. He's going to *FLIP* when he sees you." Pin couldn't contain the smile that was spreading across his features now. Finally, there was at least some good news in all this. Some sense of hope.

At first, Sarah paused at the mention of her husband's name, and then fresh tears started to run down her face as she covered her mouth to keep from making too much noise. Molly spoke before she could. "You mean— Daddy is okay...?" The way she asked made it seems as if she was afraid of what the answer might be. She had asked her mother a similar question at least a dozen times, and she could never get a straight answer.

Pin nodded with the biggest smile. "Yeah, and he's stronger than ever! Come on. We're all meeting back up at the inn. Knowing him, he's probably there by now." He moves out of his kneeling position and stands up fully. He reached his hand out and proceeded to help Sarah and Molly up to their feet as well. "There are still *a lot* of monsters out there, so you guys have to stick close to me—"

Before he could finish the sentence, there was a loud scream at the door. "HELP ME!" A man screamed. "PLEASE HELP ME!"

The loud pleas immediately put Pin on edge again. He could understand being scared, but didn't this guy realize that he was going to lead the demons straight here? He whispered to Sarah and Molly. "Stay here. Don't move." Pin turned and rushed to the door. He could only hope that there wasn't a legion of demons waiting for him on the other side. When he got to the front of his shop, he saw the man through the glass window of the entrance. He looked pale and absolutely terrified. The man yelled again. "PLEASE HELP ME!"

Pin attempts to shush him from the other side of the door. "Hey, calm down. You're going to attract more of them." He fumbled a little as he worked to unlock the door and open it. His hands were so jittery that even the simplest tasks took longer than expected. "Quick, come inside. You're safe—"

But Pin's sentence stopped there, with his voice getting caught in his own throat. There at the door was the man that was screaming for help, but it was only the top half of his body. His bottom half, from the waist down, looked to have been cut clean off and instead replaced with many dozens of large spider-like legs. It was as if a demon had buried itself inside him in the same manner that a hermit crab does a new shell. Pin hadn't noticed it through the window, but now that he had a good look at him, the man moved like a puppet on strings. There was nothing here that was akin to realistic human motor skills. It was clear the man had long since been dead, and his corpse was being used as a lure by the demon. "HELP ME!" The limp body of the man yelled.

Horrified, Pin tried to quickly close the door, but it was too late. The monster forced its way in, practically tearing the shop's door off its hinges. The force of which knocked Pin back and caused his head to slam into the hardwood floor. His vision went blurry, and his head immediately started to throb in pain. He didn't have much time to recover though, as he could see the blurry figure of the demon barreling towards him.

He managed to harness a fire spell in his hand and used it to blast the creature back just before it was about to attack him. The beast was sent hurling away and broke through the door frame of the shop. The thing rolled on the ground as it tried to put the fire out but never could. There was a horrible scream that was a mixture of both man and beast as it steadily burned alive from the magical fire.

He knew the commotion would trigger the curiosity of the other demons in the area though, so he gathered himself and got to his feet so he could go back to where Sarah and Molly were. "Guys! Come on, we—we have to go! We have to get out of here."

The night spent trying to avoid these creatures with her daughter in tow had clearly taken its toll on Sarah. She didn't move. She just stood there with a blank expression. "Go where, Pin...?" she asked, her tone sounding hauntingly bored considering the dire circumstances they were in. "Where are we supposed to go?" She stood there, her gaze staring off into space toward the front of the shop.

At first, he thought she had zoned out, but when he turned around to follow where she was looking, he could see at least a dozen red eyes peering at them through the darkness from outside. It was already too late to leave.

Molly had her arms wrapped around her mother's waist, crying about how scared she was, and at that moment, Pin had the realization that Sarah was right. There were too many of them. There was no place that was safe in this town now, and the shocking revelation that none of them were going to survive the night became increasingly clear.

He was so tired of fighting. Part of him wanted to just curl into a ball and get the whole thing over with. But, when he glanced at Sarah and Molly, he thought of Eldridge. He couldn't imagine the unbearable pain he would feel from never having had the chance to see them again.

Pin took a deep breath. "It's okay. It's okay... everything is going to be alright." He wondered briefly if the words he was saying were more meant for the two of them or himself. He helped them to go back into the closet and shut the door again. "Just stay in here, okay? And just—just don't come out. Ever. Not until sunrise..."

"Pin... what are you going to do?" Sarah asked.

"I'm not really sure, to be honest..." he felt weak, drained, and dizzy. There was no doubt that he had a concussion, and his ability to conjure more spells was almost depleted. There was only so much magical energy he could use in a day, and he had almost used it all up by now. His only plan was to keep firing as many fire spells as he could until they eventually overtook him. He figured he would kill a few of the monsters that way at least, and maybe they wouldn't notice Sarah and Molly still hiding in the closet because of it.

He walked into the main area of the store just as three bestial four-legged demons started to come in. *Alright, Pin... this is it,* he thought to himself. He readied the fire spell in his hand as he walked forward, but he nearly tripped when he bumped into the bag of potions he was carrying before. He couldn't believe he had almost forgotten that was there.

As the beasts closed in on him, he picked up the bag and started rummaging through the potions inside. He pulled out a pink potion and began to gulp it down quickly.

One of the bestial demons was covered in fur with legs like a grasshopper and a mouth filled to the brim with rows of teeth. It leapt toward Pin, intending to take off a limb with its sharp claws, but instead was met with a burst of fire from Pin's mouth that charred the creature to a crisp. It was enough to cause the other demons to take a few steps away from him. Seeing their reaction, he didn't hesitate to grab another potion out of the bag. This time, he grabs a vial full of blue liquid inside.

After drinking that one, his eyes glowed a bright shade of blue, and a stream of lightning fired from his pupils, electrocuting and killing the other two demons. By this point, the browsing area of his shop was partially black and burned.

Not wanting to risk starting a fire, he carried the bag of potions outside with him to confront the demons. There was a variety of different monsters awaiting him.

There were floating eyes, odd flying creatures, and beasts with large bodies that were akin to insects but had the heads of mammals. Pin spoke, "I—I don't know if you can understand me, but... I'm not going to let any of you monsters back in my shop!"

His eyes sparked blue again, and an electric bolt shot from them, frying a floating eyeball demon to a charred ball. This caused the rest of the creatures to run forward. He cast a fire spell that ended up burning several of the demons. One of the thicker-skinned ones was able to ignore the flames, though. This demon was a lizard-like creature that ran on its hind legs, and with a whip of its tail, it sent Pin hurling backwards onto the ground.

By some miracle, he had still held onto the bag. And by some other miracle, the bottles of potions inside were not broken when his body crashed into the ground. He had to be more careful, he thought. If he

CHAPTER SIX

lost access to the bag, he knew it would quickly be over for him. He saw the lizard creature charge at him again, and this time when he reached into the bag, he pulled out a vial of teal-colored liquid. After drinking it, Pin spat at the monster just as it was about to bite him. This caused the demon to reel back. Pin's spit was like acid now, and the creature shrieked from the saliva burning through the flesh of its skull. It tried to wipe it off to no avail, only achieving to rip the skin from its face with its claws. Its eyes started to liquefy and drip down its face akin to bloody, fleshy tears, leaving only empty eye sockets in their wake.

Its body would fall down with a thud while more demons charged at Pin. The monsters were as plentiful as they were horrifying, but each were being met with a similar fate as the previous ones. Burnt to ash, electrocuted, dissolved. But even more were coming. When he killed enough to give himself a little reprieve, he cast a spell of protection around himself, causing a faint glow of yellow to flow across his brown skin. It was the same one he used to shield himself from the Magic Bomb explosion prior, and while it wasn't very good, it would at least protect him a little bit from harm.

And he would need it because he had never seen creatures act in the manner that they did. Even as their brethren were dying right beside them, they never stopped their assault. It was like they didn't even care about their own well-being.

Over time, Pin's muscles began to ache, and his movements started to slow. Demons were beginning to get close enough to do damage to him in spite of the spell. He got cuts, bruises, and bite marks even through his partially damaged gambeson.

Even with the potions, the thought of putting a stop to them before he received a serious wound was becoming less likely. But he had the thought that maybe he could lead them away from the shop, so he started to run from them instead. While the plan worked, and the legions of demons gave chase, he was so tired that he knew he wasn't going to be able to get very far. Maybe a couple of blocks at best before his legs would give out. He reached into the bag and grabbed the last potion that was left. A small vial of purple liquid. It was a potion that was requested by the occasional mage traveler that strolled into town.

The potion gave an absurd level of magical power to the point that it would risk damaging the organs of someone who wasn't experienced enough to handle it. He wasn't sure if he could, but with little choice left now, he drank down the whole potion in one gulp. It was disgusting. In fact, he almost vomited just from the taste alone.

But it worked. He immediately felt an insane surge of energy flow through him. His hands started to glow even without the need to focus or conjure a spell. It felt great at first, but it quickly started to feel overwhelming, like the feeling of having stuffed yourself full of your favorite meal too fast.

Trying to contain the surge of magic alone was enough to bring him to his knees. There was far less distance between him and the demons than he had thought, and they caught up to him much faster than he anticipated. In seconds they were biting and clawing through his gambeson as well as other parts of his body that weren't protected. Flesh was ripped from him as he became covered in deep cuts and bites until he was drenched in his own blood.

He was on the verge of slipping into unconsciousness when he conjured his last spell. He had this surge of power in him, but he was so weak and so tired that he didn't fully realize what he was casting. So many spells that he had studied flashed into his mind in quick succession before he unleashed the power of the potion he had drank.

A bright glow was emitted from his body which was quickly followed by an eruption of blue flames that burst forth like an explosion. The very moment any of the magical fire touched the demons, they were immediately burned to ashes. Many did not even have time to cry in pain before the hot flames took over their body and incinerated them all to

CHAPTER SIX

dust.

Pin collapsed on his back soon afterward. He was barely conscious and bleeding profusely over the ground. He struggled to even breathe. In fact, it felt harder and harder to breathe the more he tried. He felt his heart skip a beat and then skip several more after that.

His body shuddered before he could feel himself begin to convulse wildly. His eyes rolled into the back of his head, and a mixture of blood and saliva began to bubble past his lips and drip down the sides of his mouth. He felt himself go numb as what little consciousness he had faded away from him as the ground began to glow bright yellow. He only had one final thought before he blacked out completely.

Am I about to die?

CHAPTER SEVEN

Eldridge made his way back to Mace and Tulips to meet the others. Thanks to his speed, he got there much quicker than he would have otherwise, but he knew he was running out of time for the effects of the potions. By the time he got there, he saw Thorne, Alyssia, and a group of townspeople standing outside of the inn.

"Listen, I say we leave while we still can before more demons come back," someone in the crowd of townspeople said.

Alyssia chimed in. "No, please don't. There might still be more demons in the forest. Besides, Gorgron said that there was a barrier surrounding the town—"

"Gorgron?" A woman interrupted. "Who the hell is Gorgron?"

"Is she talking about that orc freak? Didn't he get kicked out already?" Another townsfolk added.

The crowd's voices had started to escalate. Thorne and Alyssia had clearly lost control of them by this point. The purposefully loud footsteps of Eldridge's armor hitting the stone road were enough to attract their attention, even before he spoke. He received many gasps with his name said several times amongst them. They had thought he was dead, along with most of the other guardsmen.

"She speaks the truth," the head guardsman said as he stepped forward. "You'll be dead long before you reach the capital." His words carried the kind of respect that caused the townspeople to immediately take heed. They whispered among themselves, but there was no protest at his words.

Thorne had the biggest grin on his face. "Heh. Looks like ye guardsmen don' have as big of a stick up ya rear end than me thought. Even got a lil' common sense too." Eldridge simply grinned back at him and regarded Alyssia, "Where is Pin? Has he gotten back yet?"

Alyssia shook her head. "No, not yet. I haven't seen Gorgron anywhere either," she said.

"Well, with what's happening to the town, we have to assume Gorgron failed somehow," Eldridge stated. "It's up to us now. We need to gather whatever supplies we can and—"

"HELP!" Sarah yelled as she ran toward the group from a couple blocks away. The blonde was pushing a wheelbarrow with what appeared to be a limp body inside, covered in blood and wounds. Molly was following behind her. "Help! We need a doctor! Please!"

Eldridge eyes widened in disbelief. "*Sarah...?*" He couldn't believe it. He wanted nothing more in the world than to give her and his daughter the biggest hug he could, but the only thing that stopped him was the glance he took down at the wheelbarrow she was pushing. The limp body inside was Pin. He couldn't even count the number of wounds and tears he had over him. His skin was turning dangerously pale. He looked like he was on death's door as the only signs of any life came from the occasional convulsion in his body. Alyssia was the first one to run over. She reacted before Eldridge even had a chance to fully process what was happening. "Oh, gods, Sarah! What happened to Pin!?" Alyssia asked before the look of horror on Sarah's face made her realize she hadn't recast her illusion spell. Sarah screamed at the top of her lungs. "M-MONSTER!!! Help me!" she screamed.

Alyssia immediately responded by casting a spell that made her appear back to her regular elf self to the blonde. "No, no, no! Not a monster! It's me, Alyssia! See? Better?"

Sarah had a look on her face that made it clear that she had never been so confused in her entire lifetime. "Wha— no! No, not better, wha— what are you—" Before she could finish, Eldridge walked up to his wife and daughter to comfort them. He wrapped his arm around his wife in a half-hug and placed his hand on his daughter's head. His daughter immediately hugged him, ignoring the heavy plated armor he was wearing. "Sarah, it's okay. I'll explain the whole thing to you later," he said. "Tell us what happened to Pin."

Seeing her husband immediately brought tears to her eyes. She couldn't help but hug him along with Molly. They both had spent so much time wondering if they were ever going to see him again. "I—I don't know what happened. He told us to hide, and then— oh, Eldridge, he went out to fight all of those monsters by himself."

"By *himself?*" he said, before quickly turning to the citizens. "Are any of you a doctor? Or a nurse? Can anyone here help him!?" He asked with urgency, but there was nothing but silence for a while. After a few seconds, one of the townspeople came forward and raised their hand. It was hard to tell what race she was, but she looked human except for her purple skin and natural green hair. She wore a simple dress, and her voice sounded modest and unimposing. "I—I know a little healing magic. Mostly for minor cuts and bruises..." she said, looking fairly unsure about volunteering for this.

"Please, anything you can do to help would be appreciated," Eldridge pleaded.

She gave a nod and went over to Pin so that she could place her hands over his chest. They began to glow a vibrant green color as she did her best to heal him.

Eldridge turned to Sarah. "Pin had a bag of potions with him. Did you see it anywhere?"

Sarah had to think for a few moments to even remember seeing anything like that. "Uuh. Oh, right!" she said. "Yeah, there was something that looked kind of like a bag near him," she continued. "It was so burnt I couldn't really tell what it was until you brought it up. The only potions I saw were a couple of empty ones lying around on the ground..."

Alyssia chimed in, "Empty!?" There was worry in her voice. "Eldridge, didn't he say you're not supposed to drink more than three potions at a time?"

It was then that Pin's body convulsed, and he spat up blood that splattered against the woman's hands who was healing him. The sudden splash of blood caused her to squeal.

Eldridge grit his teeth from stress at the state Pin was in. "Yes, he did. So what does that mean, are his organs failing!?"

"I don't know, but he had already taken two potions before you guys even showed up! He has to be over his limit by now." Alyssia felt absolutely useless. She had never practiced healing magic. In fact, the only magics she ever practiced were the ones she used to hide herself.

Thorne would make his way over after seeing how dire the situation was. "Let me see da boy," he said as he went over to the opposite side of the woman. Everyone watched closely as he stretched his hands out over Pin's chest in a similar matter as the woman across from him. He looked up at the purple-skinned woman. "What's ya name, lass?"

The woman looked visually disturbed by the sight of blood on her hand, but his voice snapped her out of it somewhat. "It's... it's Sala," she spoke those words so quietly that Thorne almost didn't hear them.

He had compassion for this woman as she obviously did not want to be in this position, but he respected her courage to do so anyway. "Listen, Sala, we're abou' ta pull this boy from the reaper's bosom. Stay focused, 'cause it's gonna take all of ya magic ta do it," Thorne said this with a sense of purpose and authority.

Sala swallows dryly in response, but she nods her head at his words.

"Gods, I know it's been years... but giv' me da gift jus' one more time." Thorne closed his eyes for a moment and prayed. Slowly, his hands gave off a glow of pure light similar to Sala's, but it was much brighter. Pin's convulsions appeared to slow, but he still remained unconscious. Deep flesh wounds started to heal themselves as if they were being stitched back together by an unknown force.

Alyssia watched on, admiring the fact that Thorne was actually using magic again. She whispered a couple of thank yous under her breath that she knew the dwarf would be too focused to hear.

Eldridge stood beside Alyssia, witnessing the event in awe with her. It was easy for a lot of townsfolk to write off Thorne's stories as fabrication, but after tonight, everyone was going to pay closer attention when he spoke. Seeing the distress that was on Alyssia's face still, Eldridge decided to offer her some comforting words. "He's stronger than you think, you know. The boy is going to pull through this," he said reassuringly.

Alyssia nodded in response, "I know he will..." For the first time that evening, there appeared to be at least some sense of calm in the town. Everyone had gathered together to watch the pair try their best to attempt to heal Pin. Some color had already began to return to his skin as he started to stabilize.

So much had been lost that night, but having everyone here together in a common concern for one of their own brought back a sense of peace that had been torn from them in such a short time span. However, they were only granted a few moments of this reprieve, as they all felt a rumble underneath their feet. It was almost akin to that of an earthquake. It caused disorientation immediately among all of them, and after a couple of moments, the vibrations intensified to the point that it was hard to keep balance. Some people were actually starting to fall over.

"Eldridge— wh—what's happening?" Sarah asked in a panic, and grabbed onto her husband to help keep her footing

"I—I don't know. I wish I—" Before Eldridge could complete his full sentence, he happened to look toward the edge of the town, where he noticed that there was a gigantic structure that was emerging out of the ground. The structural frame appeared to be that of a massive skeleton that was the size of at least several houses stacked on top of each other.

Eldridge didn't even have any words for what he was seeing. He wasn't even sure *what* he was seeing. It wouldn't take long for others to begin to take notice too, accompanied by screams and gasps of horror from the townspeople.

"WH-WHAT THE HELL IS THAT THING!?"

"Oh my god!"

"We're all going to die!"

"Run! We have to get out of here!"

Sheer panic and a sense of dread ripped through everyone that was there. Some people began to sob and cry uncontrollably, while others scattered and ran in different directions. Eldridge tried to get control of the situation, but it was too late. The sight of this ungodly terror looming off in the distance was just too much for the people to bare.

Alyssia— knowing that if they were not going to listen to Eldridge, she had no chance of calming them down— went over to Thorne instead.

"Thorne, is this what you meant? Is this the summoning?!" Alyssia questioned frantically. Thorne nodded his head, though he tried not to lose concentration on what he was doing. Beads of sweat formed on his forehead from trying to multi-task talking to her while he was healing. "Aye, lass, aye!" he said. "But it's far worse den tha'. Look at da beast's skull!"

Alyssia looked back at the skeleton and squinted, focusing her eyes carefully on the behemoth that was emerging from the ground. She noticed that the skull of the behemoth only had one eye socket. "Is that—is that a cyclops?!"

"Oh tha' pile of bones is too big to be a normal cyclops, lass. I only know ONE that's that big."

The realization of who he was referring to flooded her mind and struck her like a ton of bricks. "Oh, you have to be kidding me!" she exclaimed. "Thorne... is Nahath really bringing back Bhrog!? Is that possible?"

Thorne nodded. "Yes, lass! By yankin' his body outta the ground and pullin' his soul straight from 'ell."

"Okaaay, well, how do we stop it?!" she asked.

"It's such a massive undertakin' that it's gonna take 'im a while to complete it. Ya kill da summona' ya kill the summon."

Alyssia suddenly felt light-headed. Pin was down, Gorgron was nowhere in sight, and the townspeople were scattered. It was just her and Eldridge with no more potions left. How were they going to do this? She felt a rush of pain from her wound from earlier and clutched at her side. It wasn't bleeding anymore, but it was still sore.

Eldridge— who must've given up trying to round up the citizens— walked over. Hearing his voice kept her grounded.

"Alyssia, this is it," he said. "We have to stop Nahath *now*. If he brings Bhrog back, this town and the next few over are going to be gone before anyone has a chance to retaliate."

Alyssia felt her heart drop into her stomach, but with the two of them being the only ones capable of fighting right now, there were no other options. It was do or die. "Okay... right. Yeah, I'm ready," Alyssia looked like she was willing to charge toward the colossus, but Eldridge could tell she was still unnerved.

"Listen, if Nahath got this far, that means he killed Gorgron," he bluntly stated. "And I don't have much time before my potions wear off..." he lifted the faceplate from his helmet up so she could clearly see his face. She could see the determination in his eyes, but she could also see the sense of dread spread across his features. "I know this isn't easy to hear, but most of this is going to be on you, Alyssia. You're the *only* one in Green Haven that has a chance of killing him now. I'm counting on you."

The amount of pressure being put on her at that moment was crushing and overwhelming. But, in the midst of it all, there was also a sense of peace that she hadn't felt in a very long time. Never in her life had anyone put that amount of faith in her. Especially not since being cursed. The uneasiness she felt before was still there, but she had a renewed sense of conviction about what she had to do. The illusion spell she put up started to fade, revealing her more monstrous form. Her fangs were bared as she started to snarl. "I promise you. I'll do it. I'll kill him."

Eldridge nodded and put down his faceplate again. "I'm taking point," he said. Not wanting to waste time, he utilized the full agility of the speed potion that was still in his system. She had almost forgotten that Pin had given that to him, so the shock of seeing him move so fast delayed her for a second.

But she quickly got down on all fours and sprinted off behind him.

"Give 'em 'ell Alyssia!" She heard Thorne say just as she took off into the distance. Bhrog's body was being resurrected at the edge of town near where his axe's blade was buried into the ground. Alyssia felt her heart pump with adrenaline as she struggled to keep up with Eldridge. It was incredible how quickly he had adjusted to these powers and even more impressive how he dispatched any lingering demons that were between them and Bhrog's giant skeleton. She felt frighteningly small the closer they got to it. It was like seeing a mountain in the distance but not knowing how much smaller you were comparatively until you got closer.

From the angle she was at, she started to see that the skeleton was beginning to grow flesh, with muscle forming and overtaking the bones bit by bit. And at the very base of the large behemoth, stood Nahath. Various demons all surrounded him. He took notice of the two approaching. "Eldridge, my old friend!" Nahath yelled. "Is this the army you have brought to defeat me?" the ex-mayor said mockingly to the guardsmen.

Eldridge was not deterred, however. Instead, he used his lance to thrust through a demon, ripping it in half. "This is all the army we need!" he yelled back.

It was just then that the ground appeared to swell a couple yards in front of Nahath, and a giant worm demon, burst forth from it. Alyssia recognized it as the same one that attacked them back at the house. The former mayor laughed. "You are going to die out here, my old friend."

"Where's Gorgron!?" Alyssia shouted. Nahath looked nearly nothing like she remembered by this point. If it wasn't for his voice, she might not have even thought it was him. In response to the question, Nahath drifted his pointer finger off toward a vague direction. "Depends on where you look," he said.

When Alyssia's eyes followed where he was pointing, she almost gasped at what she saw. It was the disembodied head of Gorgron on the ground. It looked as if it had been ripped from his shoulders. There were crows with red eyes eating and picking at it with their beaks, taking bits of skin off at a time. "Oh. And there's a bit of him over there too," the next place Nahath pointed to had the orc's limbs lazily tossed into a pile with bite marks and bits of flesh missing

"All of this talk about 'The Wise One' and this is all it amounted to. Ripped apart by demons."

As Alyssia looked around, she was mortified by the sight of what was once Gorgron. Arms, legs, torso. All lazily thrown about like sacks of useless meat. She hadn't known him very well, but the thought occurred to her that she had misjudged him. He never asked for anything or expected much from anyone, but he still gave his life to protect these people. Why would he be so selfless?

Eldridge was quick to notice that she started to slow down and lose some of the zeal she had before. He called out her name as he pierceed through another demon. Nahath was starting to actively send them their way now. "Alyssia!" Eldridge said. "Stay focused! Don't let him rattle you!" His words had shaken her back to attention.

"I know, I know!" Alyssia yelled back. She felt beyond stupid that she let Nahath get in her head, even for a moment. She ran forward as more demons started to gather. There weren't as many as there were before, but there were still dozens of them.

"I figured I would face at least some opposition," Nahath said, giving a gesture toward two dozen or so of the hideous beasts that surrounded him. They immediately responded to his will, rushing toward the pair. "Which is why I put up the barrier. I couldn't risk another traveler ruining everything."

Alyssia was outright ignoring Nahath by this point. She focused on ripping and tearing through the demons he had sent her way. A couple she could kill without issue, but two dozen coming at them all at once was almost too overwhelming. Thankfully, Eldridge was there. He was masterful. The way he tossed his lance and speared through at least six demons all at once was incredible. It frees up the opportunity for her to put her claws and fangs to good use.

She opened her jaws wide enough that she was able to bring her sharp fangs crushing down on an eyeball demon, causing blood to splatter in every direction. At the same time, her claws dug into the side of a four-legged beast that had curved, jagged horns. She ripped open the creature's side, its innards spilling onto the ground. After the monster fell, she broke its horns off and used them to stab and gouge other demons to rip them asunder. Her fur splashed with fresh coats of blood all over again.

Killing these demons was becoming more natural than she ever wanted it to be. It was like a reflex by this point. Blood began to fill her nostrils while a small horde of demons ripped at her body, creating gashes and deep wounds throughout. She started to lose herself in the midst of the carnage. There was an overpowering, primal need to survive that swept over her. This was barbarity over strategy. Savagery rather than skill. Her mind slipped into a different state of consciousness.

The only thing she remembers after that was being hunched over one of the last demons that attacked her. It had basically been reduced to a pile of butchered flesh. Her heart was pounding in her chest as she stood there covered in cuts and bruises.

CHAPTER SEVEN

She then heard Nahath's voice. "When you fight, you become like a rabid dog, you know that? You really are just like these demons, aren't you, Alyssia?" he said.

"I'm not a demon..." Though Alyssia barely recognized her own voice at that moment. Her fangs were bared as she growled with blood dripping from her maw. The irony was that she couldn't see how indistinguishable she was from the monsters she was killing.

"Then why didn't you notice Eldridge's potion had run out?" Nahath questioned.

Alyssia's eyes snapped open. When she looked off to where she saw him last, she could see an unconscious Eldridge in the mouth of a demon that stood on two legs. It had no arms, but it had a large mouth with sharp fangs. The only thing that kept its bite from penetrating through him was his armor. But even that started to give as deep dents began to form in the metal. She rushed over as quickly as she could, grabbing the demon's mouth and prying it open to the point that its jaw was snapped out of place. It fell to the ground, yelping like a harmless puppy.

Eldridge was dropped from the monster's jaws, and when she checked on him, she saw that he was still breathing, but he wasn't in the best of shape. She had to rip off his chest piece because, although the demons didn't penetrate it, they had dented the armor to the point that it was obscuring his breathing. It didn't help that he likely had a few broken ribs as well. "I'm so sorry, Eldridge..." Alyssia said. How could she not have noticed he was in trouble?

"You keep killing and maiming these demons," Nahath stated as he started to walk toward her. "But I'll just summon more. Do you really think you can win like this?" The town's former mayor had gotten so bold as to stand over Alyssia while she knelt down next to Eldridge. "Look around you..." he gestured to the ground that was still shining brightly with odd symbols that were all interconnected. "I spent more than a decade magically transcribing these patterns into the ground just for tonight."

He then made an odd gesture with his hand that she didn't recognize. And suddenly, as if being raised from the pits of hell itself, a skeletal creature started to claw its way out of the earth little by little. Its form slowly began to take on blood and flesh, with the creature looking similar to a lion, but there were no eyes or fur, and its feet had many claws on them. The demon was not hostile to Nahath and did not even give a reaction when Nahath patted its head. "Magnificent creatures, aren't they? These monstrosities from hell," Nahath said before, with a flick of his finger, the demon went back over to where some of the other demons were.

"With this summoning circle and all of the human souls that I have now, I no longer need any special rituals or sacrifices to summon demons. I can do it at will," he said. Alyssia finally understood why he was being so bold as to stand a mere few feet from her after seeing what she was able to do to his demon legion.

"You said my name..." Alyssia said as she looked up at him. "Earlier, you said my name. Have you known this was me the entire time?"

That question caused Nahath to laugh. "Of course not," he said bluntly. "I would never have allowed you to live in this town if I knew." He gets closer and squats down to be more at eye level with her. The one eye that he had left did not even look human anymore. Instead of the pupil being a perfectly round circle, it instead looked closer to a blot of ink that had been sloppily spilled from an ink bottle.

"I knew because I swallowed the eye of a demon. I can peer into your soul. I know exactly who you are, Alyssia. How did you think I saw the magic leave Eldridge's body?" He stood back up to his full height and looked back at the demons he still had left. "Go. Kill anyone that's still alive." The monsters roared in unison and rushed toward the town.

Since they all took off at once, Alyssia couldn't have stopped them, even if she tried. Not only that, but she couldn't leave an unconscious

Eldridge lying on the ground, unguarded. There was no doubt in her mind that Nahath would kill him the moment she left his side.

It was then she recalled Thorne's words. Kill the summoner, and you kill the summons. Alyssia quickly got to her feet. "I'll just kill you before your little pets can make it into town—" Before she could even finish her sentence, she saw the shadow of Bhrog's hand coming down on all of them. She didn't have enough time to react. His hand was huge. She did the only thing she could do, which was raise her arms to catch it and stop the cyclops from crushing them. It was a struggle, though. She felt like every ounce of her strength was being pushed to its limit.

Skin was finally starting to cover most of Bhrog's body by this point, although only half of him was outside of the ground. "You're not going to be able to kill me, Alyssia," Nahath said, now having gained full control of the gigantic creature.

"Screw you!" She blurted out as she felt her knees buckle under the weight. "You forgot you're under the hand too? Why don't I just let Bhrog crush us all if you're gonna kill us anyway!?"

Nahath shook his head. "You can't kill someone who's not alive to begin with," Nahath stated as he moved to place a hand on her chest just beneath her collarbone. "Even if Bhrog's hand crushes me too, I'll just reconstruct myself." Nahath's fingers gradually put more and more pressure on Alyssia's chest until his digits started to puncture her skin. Blood began to spill from the wound, along with an intense feeling of pain that made her gasp.

"After I've killed you both, I'm going to revive you two. I'll make you my left and right hand." Nahath's fingers dug inside of the wound he was making, causing Alyssia to struggle for air. Spurts of blood were now coming out of her chest. She tasted blood mixed in with her own saliva.

"The only reason you still stand now is because of your fake demon blood," Nahath said, his hand starting to disappear into her chest cavity. "You should thank whoever did this to you. That curse is the only thing about you that's noteworthy."

Alyssia could do nothing to stop the undead man from beginning to curl and clutch his fingers around her still-beating heart. "Go to hell, Nahath..." Alyssia said weakly. It was barely an audible whisper.

She expected some kind of banter back from him, but he stood there wordlessly as he started to pull on her most vital organ. It was the worst pain she had ever felt in her life. She couldn't even scream. She could only give near-breathless whimpers. Her vision went blurry, and it was only through sheer force of will that she was able to keep from passing out.

He pulled hard at her heart and ripped it out from her chest, causing blood to spill out like a waterfall over her own body. Because the anatomy of a demon was different from that of an elf, the thick blood vessels and arteries that connected her heart to her body were still attached. Nahath admired the heart in his hand. He watched it beat and still try to pump blood through the rest of her body. "It's admirable, you know," Nahath said while he started to put pressure on her heart. Alyssia's body shook uncontrollably.

She felt so cold. But she remained on her feet, arms still raised to keep Bhrog's hand at bay. "It's amazing that you stay on your feet, still trying to keep Bhrog from crushing the both of you. Despite your heart being ripped out, you continue to stubbornly struggle." Nahath placed his other hand over the heart, feeling every tremor that rippled through it as it pumped. "When I bring you back as my minion, I can only hope your tenacity carries over." He moved to apply enough pressure on the heart to crush it, but... it kept its form. He attempted to crush it again with the same result.

It was only after examining further, that he realized there was a very faint glow coming from the organ itself. It had a protective spell placed on it, but it was an extremely basic one. Elementary even. So pathetic that he couldn't help but laugh again. "Wow. You're full of surprises aren't you, Alyssia?" Nahath asked, admiring the only thing that protected her heart from him. "But isn't this the same basic protection spell little elf girls use to protect their baby dolls? Is the only magic you really know as an elf, just the ones you use to mask yourself?"

Even as Nahath mocked her, Alyssia was completely unresponsive to him. It took everything she had to keep herself standing. Her eyes were beginning to gloss over as blood dripped from her mouth and chest. She felt herself slip closer and closer to death, and that weak protection spell she cast on her heart was already starting to show cracks from the pressure that Nahath was applying to it. It would break before long. Her vision had long since blurred, and she could feel that her arms and legs were going to give out involuntarily due to the severe lack of blood flow coursing through her veins.

She could see Nahath's mouth moving. He was still speaking to her, but her mind was in such a fog that she couldn't fully comprehend all the words.

It was in that moment, at death's door, that out of the corner of her eye, she noticed something strange. Her vision was hazy, but she could swear some of the old blood stains that had splattered all over the ground were becoming fresh and red again, as if being given life anew. The blood then started to get thick, almost to the consistency of syrup, but it still flowed and rippled like blood would. The disembodied body parts that she observed on the ground from before all started to move and get pulled in together.

It was almost a blessing that she was so close to dying with her skin turning pale and her eyes dulled over. She didn't even have the strength left within her to fully process or express shock anymore. Because if she could, she would have given away what was happening right behind Nahath.

Gorgron was beginning to reform.

His limbs began to reconnect to his torso after being pulled in place by his own blood. Crows that had started to pick at his eyes began to scatter when his head was pulled by the strange blood and reconnected to the rest of him. He was all back in one piece now. It was like some kind of twisted miracle when the orc was able to get back up to his feet again. But something wasn't quite... right about it.

One of his arms and one of his legs looked like they were put back together wrong, like some kind of poorly repaired toy. His arm was twisted backward, and one knee was bent the wrong way. It was as if a child had tried to hastily repair one of their favorite dolls.

The matter of which he walked made it look like he was some kind of puppet on strings as he hobbled his way forward. His face had bits of flesh eaten off of it from the crows, and one of his eyes was hanging from its socket, half picked apart as well.

Nahath hadn't even noticed the orc was behind him until it was too late. The orc's large hands closed in around Nahath's head, causing him to let out a wail in surprise. Nahath's skull erupted into green flames the moment he got a hold of him, causing the rest of the flesh and hair that was on his head to be burnt away.

"*Gorgron*!?" Nahath yelled. His hands attempted to pull away the orc's grip, but he was far too strong for the mayor to do anything.

"The Wise One has chosen to bless you on this day," Gorgron said just before he bared his teeth and pulled upward on his skull. "He has decided to free your soul from this decrepit body."

Alyssia watched as Nahath's head and spine was slowly dislodged from the rest of his frame. Nahath fought against the orc the entire time. He was making a vain attempt to stop what was inevitably about to happen. "*You're making a mistake*! You don't know what you're do—" Nahath suddenly gave a sickening shriek as his skull and spine were torn from the rest of him. His body fell limp to the ground and started to quickly lose any color or resemblance of life that it had mere moments ago.

It was like his very soul had left the vessel. Decay started to take effect all at once. Maggots began to form and feed off the darkening flesh of

Nahath's vessel, and now that the summoner had been killed, the mighty titan, Bhrog had started to fade away into dust in the breeze.

"Even horrible sinners are given grace through The Wise One's mercy," Gorgron said as he watched the maggots devour and eat what remained of Nahath.

Alyssia fell to her knees, barely alive. Her heart was still outside of her body when Gorgron made his way to her. He knelt down beside her. "You will not die here..." the orc said, his hand coming up to touch her forehead. His large palm blocked her vision, and she could feel herself starting to pass out. The last thing she heard was his voice comforting her in the midst of unconsciousness.

"The Wise One has plans for you..."

EPILOGUE

Pin's eyes snapped open, and he sat up swiftly. He quickly realized that he was lying in a bed in one of the rooms of Mace and Tulips. His glasses weren't on, so he instinctively reached for the nightstand only to realize that they were not there. Memories started to flood his mind all at once, and he realized he'd lost them when he got put into that monster's stomach.

His own empty stomach rumbled and was accompanied by a throbbing headache. He rested his face in his palms as he tried to console the throbbing in his head. Not long afterward, he heard Alyssia's voice.

"PIN!?" She practically yelled in surprise, which ignited his headache anew. She went over to sit on the bed and give him a hug, but she was not the monstrous creature he saw the other night. She looked like her normal self. Well. At least the her he was used to seeing. "I can't believe it! You're awake!" she said cheerfully.

"I don't even... remember how I get here." He realized now that his throat was very dry, and his voice came out hoarse. It was as if his vocal cords were getting used to being used again.

"Pin, you've been out for days," Alyssia said. "Thorne healed you the best he could, but we weren't sure you were gonna make it..."

He looked a little perplexed. "Thorne did?" he said with the faintest bit of surprise in his voice. He then chuckled. "I guess he wasn't joking about being a cleric, huh? With how many potions I drank... I really should have been a goner." It was a miracle, really. Those final moments before he passed out were some of the scariest seconds of his life. The horrible feeling of not knowing whether or not he was going to wake up again still sent a chill down his spine.

"Yeah... Thorne was incredible that night. He helped a lot of people." There was a small pause from her, "Oh, and make sure to thank a woman named Sala too. She and Thorne worked together that first night to get you stable."

Pin nodded. But, now that he thought about it, there was still something odd here, "Wait. Hold on. What happened to Nahath? Are all the demons just gone now?"

Alyssia smiled brightly. "Yup! We took care of it," She exclaimed. "A good chunk of that was thanks to you. There were people in hiding that said they saw you take on dozens of those things by yourself and *won!* You're a hero, Pin!"

Pin blushed and rubbed the back of his head sheepishly. "A hero...?"

"Yeah! Everyone was talking about it. Especially Sarah and Molly! They said you were all like—" She clears her throat and puts on an overly deep heroic-like voice. It sounded nothing like Pin's. "'Stay in the closet and don't come out!'"

Pin's embarrassment only deepened. "I mean... it didn't go *exactly* like tha—"

Before he could finish his thought, Alyssia interrupted him. "Everyone is touting you as the town's first real mage!" she exclaimed as she got to her feet. "You actually woke up just in time too! Thorne has been making breakfast for everyone every morning since that night. We've all been working hard to— well—to rebuild," she said.

This all felt so surreal to him, but Pin nodded. "Okay. I'll be right down." But then he paused. "Hey, Alyssia..." he said, his voice trailing off a bit.

"Yeah?" She responded curiously.

"We didn't have time to discuss it that night, but—I wanted to ask...

um." Pin stuttered a little. He wasn't sure exactly how to bring up her curse in a tactful way. Luckily for him, Alyssia seemed like she caught on to what he was trying to say.

"You mean about the curse?" she asked.

"Yeah... How did it happen?"

Alyssia looked visibly a little uneasy. It was not that she didn't want to tell the story, but actually discussing it was something that was so out of the ordinary, she wasn't sure how. She spent a significant amount of time trying to hide it.

"Well... long story short? I used to be a high-born elf. Silver spoon and all that," she started. "And I was every bit the stereotype. I was pompous, full of myself, and—I won't sugar coat this—I looked down on people, Pin. And after mistreating people for so long, you eventually might mistreat the wrong person. Like a person that can curse you for the rest of your life." While visibly she still looked uncomfortable, it did feel like a burden had been lifted off of her shoulders.

Pin listened attentively, but the story made him rather anxious as well. He and his family had always practiced clean, by-the-book magic. He actually didn't even know it was possible to curse someone with magic to such a degree.

"So... then why do you still keep the red skin? Why bring attention to yourself?" he asked.

She sighed in response. "No matter how good I've gotten at transmutation and illusion magic, I can never appear completely normal. It's part of the curse. I will always look red no matter what race or form I pick..."

"Geez..." Pin said as he rubbed the back of his head in a nervous habit. "I'm sorry to pry, Alyssia. Maybe I shouldn't have even brought it up."

Alyssia smiled. "No, I'm actually glad you did. It feels nice to get it off my chest, actually." She pat him on the head. "I'll see you at breakfast, but don't take too long, okay? Everyone is going to be excited to see you."

Pin smiled back at her and nodded. "Yeah, I'll be right down in a minute." Then he paused. "But can I ask one more question?"

"Yeah, anything," she replied.

"If you were that strong... why didn't you come to the forest with us?"

Alyssia stopped and swallowed dryly. It was this question that she had been fearing the most. "I— I should have...." she admitted. "I was afraid to. I was afraid of being... found out." Her gaze shifted toward the floor. "And I thought if I stayed... maybe I could help protect the people here if any more demons got through..."

Pin stayed silent for a while. And then he let out a sigh. "Oh..."

Her expression softened and became a bit sorrowful. "Do you think that makes me terrible?"

Pin shook his head in response. "No. I think— I think you were right. If you hadn't been in town, you would've died too. And you wouldn't have been there to help me." He shifted focus to her, giving her a smile again. "I'm just happy we're still alive."

Alyssia smiled back at him and wiped a tear that had made its way down her cheek. "Me too, Pin... me too"

Soon after that, Alyssia left the room. And it was around twenty minutes later that Pin finally made his way downstairs. As he came down, he noticed that the bar was absolutely packed. It looked like almost every single person who had survived that night was here.

Thorne was the first person to see Pin making his way down and decided to cheer, raising a mug of ale up into the air. "AYE! Thars Sleepin' Beautae!" he yelled. When the other townspeople noticed that he was coming down the stairs too, they cheered as well and clapped for him. It kind of took him by surprise. He was not used to having so much attention put on him at once and it showed. He looked dumbfounded.

"Come on down, Pin. Don't be shy." Pin heard Eldridge's voice coming from across the bar. He was sitting in a wooden wheelchair with basic clothing and no armor on for once. His arm was in a sling, and his body looked covered in bandages. He was there with Sarah and Molly, and they all looked happy to see him. It made him smile to know they were okay too.

Pin came down the steps but would soon have Thorne— who was standing on a bar stool—wrap his arm around his neck and pull him into a friendly headlock. From the smell of his breath and clothes there was no doubt that he was drunk already. "AYE, LAD! Let us 'ear it right from da horse's mouth! What did ya say to Sarah and Molly!?" He shouted right next to Pin's ear, which made him flinch from the loud noise. "'Stay in the closet and don't move'!?" The way he said it was in a similar way that Alyssia had said it earlier.

How long had they been talking about this? Pin couldn't have looked more embarrassed, nor could he have blushed any harder than he was now. Everyone in the bar was laughing and telling their own variation of what Pin did and how he fought the demons. Some people said that he used a vast array of spells. Some say he barely used any spells and actually fought a good amount of them with his bare hands and healing potions alone. It was the kind of good time these people needed after experiencing so much heartache only a few days prior.

Alyssia had made her way over to the doorway of Mace and Tulips, smiling while watching everyone have a good time. It looked like a return to form, and it was nice seeing Pin get so much praise for what he did.

She thought about how Nahath was wrong about a lot, but he was right about what he said to her regarding Pin. The other night he proved he didn't need any protection. He was just fine on his own.

Quietly, she left the inn, slipping out before anyone fully noticed she was gone. She walked along the cold stone streets of Green Haven. The town that was once so homely and welcoming, was now full of signs of destruction from a few days ago. Houses were broken and destroyed. There were still stains of blood here and there that hadn't been fully cleaned yet. It looked like a much different place now... But they would rebuild. They would start over. They would reform Green Haven. She found herself near the edge of town where Bhrog's giant axe resided.

However, there in the distance, and to her surprise, she saw Gorgron again. She hadn't seen him since that night, and it looked like he was about to leave. She rushed over to him. "Gorgron!" she yelled out. He stopped mid-stride and turned to look at her. He looked as if he was back to his old self again. No limbs turned the wrong way, or bits of his flesh missing. It was like the other night hadn't even happened.

"Ahh, Alyssia. You are in good spirits," the orc said as he regarded her. "But, I see you put up your illusion again."

Her mouth twisted when he mentioned her spell. "It's just... easier." Alyssia remarked. "I think the people want to do their best to forget about that night. And so do I, to be honest..." she still shuddered every time she even had the faintest thought of remembering her heart being pulled from her chest

"Nevertheless... The Wise One has rewarded your efforts to protect these people with the gift of life. You should cherish it. Praise his name from here to the highest of heavens..."

Alyssia didn't seem very willing to 'praise his name from the highest of heavens' like he said. In fact, she started to frown. "What did you—" she paused and decided to rephrase her question, "What did *The Wise One* do to Nahath? He said he couldn't be killed."

For the first time since she had known him, she saw the orc let out a hearty laugh. "You must have forgotten! The Wise One purified his soul. He released him from his mortal coil." The orc said, continuing further. "His soul was imprisoned in his body. The Wise One worked through me to relieve him so he could have eternal rest."

Alyssia didn't respond to that. She wasn't sure if she even believed it. The way Nahath screamed when he was being 'freed' didn't sound anything remotely like resting in peace.

Her forehead furrowed while she stared at Gorgron for a few moments before she allowed her illusion and transmutation spell to fade away to reveal her actual true form. She looked much the same as she did on that night, but she pointed to the middle of her chest where there was a hand-sized gaping hole where Nahath had left his mark on her still. In the center of it was her heart. It was fully exposed, but not bleeding. In fact, there didn't seem to be any damage to it from leaving it unprotected against the elements. However, there was a glisten of purple that would flash in the sunlight sometimes. She knew there had to have been a magical barrier that stayed around her heart to keep it safe. It was the only reason she hadn't dropped dead yet.

"And what about this, huh? When does The Wise One fix this? When does it heal?"

There was just a long pause from Gorgron. An uncomfortably long pause. She then saw him smile from underneath his hood. It was an unsettling smile. The kind that made her skin crawl. Eventually, he spoke. "You are in The Wise One's gentle hands now," he said, his voice becoming increasingly giddy as he spoke of his god. "He's given you life anew... But he can take it away at his leisure." The orc removed his hood to show her his fully scarred face and his overly cheerful expression. "Does that not make you excited?"

This whole conversation was making her feel ill and deeply disturbed. "What are you even talking about!? I don't want to 'owe' him anything. I want—"

"—to die." Gorgron said as if completing her sentence for her. The abruptness took her by surprise. She couldn't even get any words out.

Gorgron started to approach her, which made her instinctively take several steps back to create distance between them. "Yes. Yes, I understand now. You want to die. You want The Wise One to take back his mercy because you feel you are *unworthy* of it." In spite of what he was saying, there was no malice or signs of sarcasm in his voice. He looked like he genuinely believed every word he was speaking to her. He stretched out his hand as if he was going to place it on her forehead like a priest blessing a disciple. "Yes. Please. Just renounce it. Say you renounce his mercy," he continued. "Your heart will spill from your chest, and you will pass away gently in a puddle of your own blood."

Alyssia was horrified. Why did she feel like he was getting some kind of sick pleasure from all of this? Her legs wouldn't move, and she didn't dare lay a finger on him. She was sure if she hurt him in any way, 'The Wise One' would take back the 'blessing' he gave her.

"Wh— *what does he want from me?!*" She yelled in a panic. It caused Gorgron to stop and look confused all of a sudden. He looked as if she was the odd one. As if she had changed her convictions in the blink of an eye. He withdrew his hand. "Even I do not know. The Wise One only reveals his purpose in due time. Even to his most faithful." He put his hood back on and turned away from her.

"If we ever cross paths again, The Wise One will reveal his path for you." He started to walk away, leaving her standing there in the field. "For now, enjoy your life. Embrace it. You will never know when the time will come that The Wise One will ask for repayment for his blessings."

As he started to disappear into the forest, Alyssia stood there, stunned. She was about to say something, but anything she wanted to say got stuck in her throat. She didn't know if she even *wanted* to converse with the orc anymore. In fact, a large part of her was very glad to see him finally leave.

But, with this hole still in her chest, she had to come to the horrifying and unsettling conclusion that she would see him again.

END

About The Author

Khris Smith is a fantasy writer who has a passion for all things nerdom. After many years of gaming, RPGs and tabletops, he was inspired to craft worlds of his very own full of adventures and lore. His dream is for people to become immersed in his stories just like he has been immersed in countless other tales throughout the years.

You can find me on Twitter:
@OnlyKhrisSmith

If you enjoyed Gorgron the Dark Mage and want to show your support, please consider leaving a review on Amazon and Goodreads.

ACKNOWLEDGMENTS

Special thanks to my wife and family. Your support has been everything.

In memory of Tito Maree and Dillion "Vyni" Milos

"With man this is impossible; but with God all things are possible."
- Matthew 19:26

Made in the USA
Coppell, TX
18 September 2023